I0519550

Belonging Places

*Every woman's story on life,
learning and love*

MARYANN WESTON

DEDICATION

For Jane, my sister.

Belonging Places

She sat on the deserted swing, and looked at the hills beyond.

Skylines beckoned, faint hints of times to come,

writing their messages in a cloudy future;

that unknowable place she belonged.

She swung back and forth, remembering the worn out saying;

swings and roundabouts. Her old friend whispered,

telling her to avoid a foot in a trap and swinging high,

losing her place, her face amid strangers,

who were only playing, after all.

With head held high, strong stride, sidestepping old games,

she found her will to move forward,

out of the shadows and into the clear light.

Where she could see as she walked, and know

her own name, perhaps for the first time.

She came to her belonging place then, and no-one could doubt

the tracks her journey left, visible like scars

that told the world, she'd gotten off the ride,

and would chart her own path now, belonging, not backing out

of the contract she made with herself.

CONTENTS

BOOK 1

LILIANA'S STORY

1 JOURNEYS

Liliana brushed her long, brown hair off her face and gazed dreamily out the window. Behind the thick pane of glass the countryside whirred by – green trees and order were giving way to the yellow straw colour of freshly harvested wheat crops. The sheep were already beginning to eat the stubble. Everything in the country was about use and reuse. Everything was valued, accounted for, and had a place. Unlike her.

It hadn't taken much to get her to leave her home in Sydney. She hardly ever saw her mum anymore and the reality was they just didn't connect. If they ever had, it was long, long ago, when Liliana was a child. She always liked to think her mum would have given her those giant cuddles and would have planted copious kisses on her baby cheeks…but she knew that probably wasn't the truth.

Liliana did have one fond memory – the day she was beaten up at school. When she came home with her bloodied lip to show her mum what 'they' had done to her, her mum had responded with uncharacteristic tenderness. Sitting down so she was at eye level, she had held Liliana's head between her hands and said: "Girl, don't you ever let those bastards win. Alright? You fight back, you hear?" And then she had begun to sob in Liliana's ear, deflated and defeated, the black circles under her eyes deepening to a purple colour before Liliana's child eyes.

As Liliana grew up and didn't need caring for as much, her mum came home less and less. It wasn't unusual for her mum – everyone called her Mrs Smith – to do a runner with a man she'd met at the local pub. Eventually she stopped coming back at all when Liliana was 16. And that was a relief for Liliana.

Of course the neighbours in her rundown apartment block in Blacktown tried to help, but she invented an aunt, pretending to speak to her 'aunt' loudly at night; shutting them all out. With enough invention and cold shouldering they left her alone, probably reasoning that she was, after all, 16 years old and eligible to leave school and go to TAFE or get a job. Well that's what Liliana did. She went to TAFE, but not to do a typing course like most girls in her school year; she went there to get her Higher School Certificate. With the help of a few caring teachers, Liliana finished school and enrolled in the University of Western Sydney. Of course it wasn't as prestigious as getting accepted by Sydney University with a tremendously high score, but her pass enabled her to get into a Bachelor of Librarianship and she was very happy about that, because books were Liliana's life.

For as long as she could remember, she had immersed herself in other people's words, and worlds. The grimy, yellow walls of her flat, and the mildew growing on her bathroom ceiling, couldn't contain her fiery imagination. She left her life far behind when she travelled with the characters that inhabited those pages. At first she learned all about England through the eyes of a 12 year old heroine who had magical powers and lots of friends. Bethany Flint became Liliana's idol and she began styling her hair like Bethany – braiding the front so it didn't hang limply around her oval face. Unbeknown to her, pulling her hair back away from her face showed her eyes – almond shaped and golden, and it was a distinct improvement on the Gothic look she had been cultivating. It was around that time she added 'Flint' to her name in a tribute to her heroine; the beautiful, rich and popular Bethany Flint.

She marked her 'serious' stage at around 14 years of age with an ode to Hemingway, reading copiously and learning about cosmopolitan Paris. She took on the same joie de vivre as Hemingway after that – at once distant and detached, and passionate and life affirming at the same time.

So, as Liliana Flint-Smith and with a world of books in her head, she had progressed through her three years at university, barely there in the back of the classroom but soaking up the lectures and the knowledge of her generous tutors. Although her reports always said she needed to find her voice, Liliana let the books do the talking for her. Between her books and letting everyone else speak, she really didn't have to make much of an effort, seeing as all the people she knew – the characters in her books and the real people in the streets and at university – loved to speak...a lot! It really didn't much matter that she had little to say each day.

They got used to seeing her turn up to class, her black tights under a straight jersey skirt and large, flapping black jumper. The old Doc Martins she found in the Op shop complemented the multi-coloured, woollen cap she pulled over her long and at times, straggly hair. "Oh Liliana," she often thought to herself, as she stared back at her reflection before catching the 301 bus from Blacktown to university each morning, "who are you?" She would never spend long on this question, instead pulling her woollen cap lower, almost over her eyes, and tramping hard in her Doc Martins out the door, with enough attitude to warn off the would be bullies who were looking for easy prey on her street corner.

She loved to play little games in her mind. Sometimes she would put on a posh voice when she got on the 301. Other times she put her hair in a bun and changed her usual black, sombre Goth clothes, instead putting on a colourful skirt and heels and wearing her mum's tight fitting, blue cardigan she'd left for Liliana. Looking feminine and a bit stand-offish, the cool students in the canteen would smile at her, thinking perhaps she was redeemable after all. And some well-toned, good looking boy with his blue eyes and swept back hair would give her a look which distinctly said, 'maybe you would be worth taking to bed'. But she never kept this pretence up for long. Pretty soon she was back in black, invisible and blending into the grey winter skies that so inspired her sense of style.

Learning about cataloguing, databases and references during her Bachelor of Librarianship was pretty routine for Liliana and didn't test her maths' ability which was surprisingly strong. What she really loved was the literature major in her degree. In another lifetime she would have been a writer and studied books, but the cataloguing mattered to her too, and she felt safe in the routine-ness of being a librarian. After all, everything had a place and books needed to be in their place when they weren't in the hands of the readers. To keep them safe and preserve them for the next reader – for all the Liliana's whose world was made tolerable through the encouraging voice of the writer – inspiring with the promise of an unknown, and therefore better, landscape. That expansiveness had given Liliana hope during her short life; that there was a place in this world for her too...beyond the yellow, grimy walls of her Blacktown flat.

While other university students generally left her alone, her teachers were far more generous with their time. One particular teacher, Haricula Theodori, had taken a particular interest in Liliana. A Greek immigrant, who also knew what it was like to sit at the back of the class and be largely ignored by the world, she made a special effort to draw Liliana out whenever she could.

Liliana, of course, had a giant, girl crush on her. Hari – the shortened name she liked the class to use in her tutorials – often asked Liliana what she thought the novelists were trying to say. Liliana rarely ventured a long dissertation in those classes, but she was comforted when a few students would start nodding. That meant they agreed with her and that was something. When people agree with you, she thought, then they have listened to what you say, and Liliana was not used to people listening to her. She was a realist. She knew that shy people rarely make an impact above the egos in the crowd.

"Liliana, can I speak to you?" Hari said, one overcast, morning after class. "Are you free for a coffee?"

Liliana didn't stop immediately because she wasn't sure whether Hari was speaking directly to her or not but when Hari raised her voice: "*Liliana*, do you have a minute?" she knew her favourite teacher was talking to her directly. So, turning around, and brushing her long hair out of her face, she said: "Yes, Ms Theodori."

"Hari, Liliana. Call me Hari."

Hari's brown, round Greek eyes were full of welcome and Liliana took a few steps towards her, deciding that she would interrupt her solitary journey to the canteen to buy a baked bean sandwich for morning tea, to talk with Hari.
Hari moved toward her and touched her arm in a gesture of closeness, Liliana thought.

"I'm not in a rush, *Hari*," Liliana said.

"Great, then let's head over to the quiet coffee shop on the other side of campus – not the canteen; it's too crowded. I want to talk to you about your studies."

Liliana raised one barely visible eyebrow. "Nothing's wrong is it?" she said, starting to worry. She really needed to get through this degree. The money her grandmother had left her was starting to run out, and Mr Liazzorini from the pizza bar could only give her two shifts a week. She was tired of the endless baked bean sandwiches, eggs and mince, supplemented by loads of vegetables…because they were cheaper than meat. As she approached her final semester at university, she wanted out, and to begin her search for her 'place', she thought wryly as she fingered the corner of the books in her hands.

"Nothing's wrong at all. In fact everything is fine Liliana. I just wanted to talk with you about an Honours' year next year...in English. But more of that later when we've got that much needed coffee in our hands. I've only had one this morning and it's nearly 11 o'clock!"

She linked arms with Liliana and half propelled her towards the coffee shop. Once they were seated, she took out a piece of paper which resembled Liliana's academic transcript.

"I hope you don't mind Liliana, but I was able to access your subject marks in this English major and I have to say they are impressive."

Liliana's eyes widened and she waited for the joke to come next. When it didn't, her expression became one of puzzlement. "Ah...I'm not sure I know what you mean. I've not done that well in my English major."

Hari smiled as she took a long sip of the soy latte she had ordered. Liliana was waiting for hers to cool, a little bit nervous of testing the heat against her lips in case it spilt.

"I'm telling you Liliana, your marks are better than good and I think you have the right attitude to take on Honours...you seem to understand what the writer is actually saying...the guts of it, if you know what I mean and not what academia wants you to think. You're a complete natural and I think with a little bit of mentoring, you can make a place for yourself here."

Liliana finally took a sip of her coffee and noticed with disappointment it had gone slightly cold. "Here? Oh I don't think so...I mean I don't want to sound ungrateful, but I don't want to stay here."

Hari looked slightly puzzled, and a little bit hurt, Liliana thought.

"I'm not sure I know what you mean Liliana. What I'm offering you is a career path to perhaps, one day, lecture at this university. Perhaps *write* yourself. I really think you're capable of all this," she said, waving her arm in an expansive gesture in the general direction of the university. Liliana couldn't help smile but she quickly forced it back.

"Thank you. I really mean that, but I can't stay here. I've got to find my place and this is not it," she said. She reached into her purse and took out $3 in silver coins. She placed them on the table and bit at her lip. She really was quite nervous at having to disappoint Hari Theodori.

Hari touched her arm again. "I understand Liliana, but promise me you will think it over."

Liliana nodded before hurrying out of the coffee shop. She could still make the 301 back to Blacktown. Luckily the term was nearly over and if she arrived and departed Hari Theordori's classes on time for the next week, she wouldn't have to talk about the prospect of studying Honours. If she didn't say much at all, it would all fade into the background, and she could slip comfortably back into herself. Besides, Liliana had another plan, one that would take her away from everything she had known in her short life. Towards another place.

2 WALLANGER

Liliana had not been sorry to leave the unremarkable street in Blacktown that had been her home for most of her 21 years. She had been born outside of the city, somewhere her mother never spoke of, and she had never known her real father. Her mum had said he was a drifter, a country larrikin who would never have taken responsibility for her. She was better off without him, her mum said. After all, her mother had never known her father either. When she had ploughed through the fiction aisles of the Blacktown library, Liliana had progressed to the non-fiction shelves. Here she learnt about the welfare state and intergenerational welfare. She figured she was one of the children they were talking about in their statistics.

She had given her notice to quit the local pizza bar too, and she was sorry about that. Mr Liazzorini had been decent to her.

"Ah Liliana," he had said, shaking his head. "You can't go off to the country by yourself. Get a good man; he take care of you. And you still work here – maybe even an extra shift eh, for when the baby comes along."

Liliana had almost thrown up. She hadn't even had a boyfriend yet.

"No Mr Liazzorini. I don't want to get married. I want to go work in a library, with lots of books and take walks along the lanes, and see the beautiful sunrises and sunsets."

He handed her a bit of extra money from the till.

"Here Liliana; here is your pay and a bit extra. No

man, no money. All this talk about walking down lanes and books is not going to get you very far," he said, sighing with the weight of his 14 hour a day reality.

Liliana smiled. "Mr Liazzorini you are so generous and I am going far, you know. All the way to Wallanger Hill - it's a lovely little community, a few hours' drive from here. Out of this grey city, where everyone is just working to make a living."

He sighed. "You are not wrong there Liliana. Sometimes I think that is all I do and one day, I won't be able to do anything else but sit at that corner table and watch as my son in law does what I used to do. You know I would love to go home. To Italy. You would love my village there, and food - like you've never tasted Liliana!"

"You should go Mr Liazzorini. Really, you should go there," she said as she wrapped her long scarf around her against the cold. "Goodbye, Mr Liazzorini. I hope you find your place."

As she stared out of the train window she recalled the conversation with her old boss. The further she travelled from the city, and everything she had known, the lighter she felt. She hoped what she was feeling was real, but you never knew, she thought wryly. To her right, a herd of sheep traipsed their well worn path to the waterhole. Like Mr Liazzorini, she thought. Walking to and from the pizza bar every day, driven by his 14-hour-a-day compulsion.

She had loved shutting the door on her yellow walled, grimy flat. She had written to her mother letting her know she was moving on. To greener pastures, she had written with a smile, and she would write once she was settled. She had received a letter from her mother who was living with a miner in Mackay, Queensland. Liliana hoped she was happy. While she didn't feel love for her mother, she did feel a sense of obligation – obligation to hope she was ok, and in kind hands. That much she deserved.

There were a few stragglers in the sheep herd she

noticed – a mum and her baby lamb. The mum appeared to want to catch up to the rest, perhaps feeling insecure, Liliana wondered. The baby lamb was close to being a burden. She looked away. She didn't want to think about that lamb, or if the mother stayed or if she didn't. What would happen at nightfall when the foxes came out? She shivered and laid her head against the glass, closing her eyes. In two hours she would be at Wallanger Hill train station. There was no-one coming to meet her, just a new life.

Liliana woke to the conductor's voice. "Next stop Wallanger Hill." She got down her overnight bag with her pyjamas, change of clothes and toiletries, and then searched frantically in the luggage rack at the end of the carriage for her big, battered black bag. It had belonged to the man living next door to her in Blacktown, and when he died his sister had knocked on her door. It was something she had no use for and hoped to offload to Liliana, "Sure, I'll take it," she had told her neighbour's sister. It may have been that night when she knew she would leave the city behind. Her neighbour had not been seen for three days, and unbeknown to Liliana had been dead from a stroke all that time. She felt a sense of guilt taking that old bag, but reasoned her neighbour might be thankful at least that, unlike him, she was leaving the old high rise apartment block that had brought him no peace and a lonely death.

There it was under a sparkly new, brown case that belonged to the old farmer in moleskins and boots who was making his way towards the door picking up his shiny, new case on the way. She struggled with the weight of her own bag but shifted its load to her other hand. The overnight bag she threw over her shoulder and tucked her handbag under her other arm. Waddling with the big, battered bag, she managed to get off the train and stood quiet vacantly waiting for a minute before she remembered that no-one was picking her up. She flicked her long brown hair back and raised her chin ever so slightly into the air, aware the station master was looking at her strangely. She walked slowly up to him, dragging the bag behind her.

"Umm, can you tell me where Worthington Street is?" she asked the man. He was middle aged, with a florid face and not at all friendly like a station master should be. He spoke to her as though he was annoyed she was there.

"Well miss, do you have anyone to pick you up - because by the size of that suitcase you're dragging about, I can't see you making Worthington Street on foot!"

She wasn't used to such straight talk from strangers and she hesitated. If she caught a taxi, she would spend what little money she had left. It had to make do until her first day of work in a week at the local library. But she didn't want to appear as though she hadn't enough money; as though she was some poor low life, blowing through town on welfare.

"Is there a bus that could take me?" she asked.
He burst out laughing, holding his stomach which was moving in unison with his shoulders.

"Ha, are you serious or delirious?" he said, giggling between the words. "The buses here only operate weekdays, and then sometimes and only from Bislington Road to the main street – not all over the town girl. Worthington Street's not on the route I'm afraid. And it's the weekend, you see."

She nodded, a faint trace of anger welling up inside. This man couldn't be more unfriendly if he tried. "Well then, I'll just have to get the taxi," she said curtly. And then when she was almost out of earshot: "And how 'bout a serving of manners, thank you!"

Liliana hurried toward the taxi rank. She didn't know where that comment had come from. She never, ever answered back, preferring to exact her revenge as an aside, or through her thoughts and looks, as shy people do. But she had chipped the station master about his manners. She didn't stop to look back and felt the thrill of fear run through her fingers. What if he came running after her, or shouted back at her? But he didn't do anything, and she felt his stare on her retreating figure as though she was the strangest thing on the planet.

Hailing the taxi, she handed over the address of her new flat to the driver. "Can you take me there?"

The taxi driver seemed nice enough. Middle aged and bearded. Liliana thought he might be a heavy drinker though. Something about the heaviness in his eyes that told her he'd been around. She'd seen that look in Blacktown, down at the parks and homeless shelters. He smiled through tired eyes at her. "Yeah, sure can," he said, and opened the boot. "Don't go liftin' that old thing," he said, pointing to her black, battered bag. "I'll do that." And he hoisted it into the opened boot. Getting back in, he put his foot on the old Ford's accelerator and pulled away from the rail station. "You new to town?" he asked, with what she would come to know as that familiar country drawl.

She nodded looking at his face through the side mirror. "Well…sort of. Why?"

He smiled slowly. "Not very trusting are you, but I s'pose I haven't introduced myself yet, have I? Must remember my manners. I'm Jimbo. Jimbo McKay. Used to be a policeman round here; well that was before I got shot…clean through my liver. Blew half of it away."

She didn't know whether to laugh or cry and wondered at the end of a long journey whether she should have stayed at Blacktown after all.

"I'm sorry to hear that," she managed, and then trying to change the subject, "I'm Liliana. Liliana Flint-Smith. From err, Blacktown Sydney. I'm the new librarian. Well I start at Wallanger Library in a week…"

Jimbo laughed again, loudly and this time his eyes lit up. "Well, Ms Flint-Smith I'm pleased to meet you. Never heard of the Flint-Smith's from Blacktown but that's a fancy name you've got," he said, chuckling as the Ford pulled into Worthington Street.

She paid the fare from what little money she had, still irritated there were no buses that ran through the street. Jimbo winked at her. "Hey, how 'bout you keep this," he said, pushing the crumpled $10 back into her hand. "Pay me back when you start that big job of yours."

She smiled then, something she didn't do often. "Thanks."

Liliana waved him off and turned around to face the square block of units in front of her. Red brick with a flat roof, but clean she reasoned and there was a small garden with trees and some lawn. She sighed with relief and looked down at the big, black, battered bag. "Come on; one last haul." She struggled with the bag for the final time she hoped, catching a fleeting glimpse in her mind's eye of the shiny brown bag the farmer had picked up from the train. One day she would buy herself one of those, she thought.

Walking slowly up the gravel driveway she searched for Unit 6, oddly her favourite number. It was the corner unit with the big Scarlet Oak in front. She touched its trunk on the way past. Her tree now, she thought. As she turned the key in the door she heard a voice nearby. Swinging around, an old woman was sitting on the veranda. It wasn't the long, white hair that caught Liliana's eye but the woman's green eyes. If ever eyes spoke a thousand words, it was these ones.

"Don't mind me," the old lady said. "I just live here."
Liliana turned to meet those eyes. "Yeah, so do I," she said.

3 STRANGE MEETINGS

She turned the latch of Unit 6 Worthington Street, confidently, despite the nosey woman sitting outside. Ignoring her, she dragged her big, black bag through the doorway and slammed it shut, almost in the old lady's face. But the lady was persistent. No sooner had Liliana put her luggage down than someone was knocking, loudly, on the front door.

Liliana raised her eyes ceiling-ward. Unbelievable!

"Hey you in the old boots and black get up. Might be neighbourly if you introduced yourself. Can't be good manners to walk straight on by," she yelled through the keyhole.

Despite herself Liliana opened the door, her face thick with the anger she felt.

"I've just arrived. I'm new to town. And I don't usually mix with strangers."

"Umm," the old lady snorted. "I'm not a stranger actually, I'm your neighbour and I'd like to welcome you to the neighbourhood *actually.*"

"But…I've not settled in," Liliana almost pleaded.

"Never mind," the lady said, pushing her way past, eyes darting about the room and, to Liliana's horror, sitting herself on the pre-furnished sofa in front of the old TV. "Like to say this is a nice place, but it's a bit…underdone," the lady said. "Name?"

Liliana's jaw just about dropped to the floor. It was a few seconds before she recovered her composure, fighting the instinct to answer back and tell the lady just what she thought about her manners...was everyone in this country town rude? Instead she swallowed hard and took a deep breath, aware this was her first day in a new town, at the beginning of a new life she...well, didn't want to mess up.

"Ah, Liliana. Liliana Flint-Smith." She waited for the cynicism that usually came when she used her double barrelled surname.

"Mmm. Interesting. Not entirely unexpected of course. My name is Danny. Danny Bourchier actually. Nice, yes and not even double-barrelled," she said, grinning like a teenager.

Despite herself, Liliana smiled and let her guard down just a bit. "Nice to meet you Danny. I don't know where the tea is, but if I can find some. Would you like a cup?"

Danny shook her head. "No Liliana. Can't stop. I'm heading off downtown to catch the supermarket before it closes. Would you like me to pick up some supplies for you?"

"What are you - a mind reader?" she said, looking at the bare cupboards.

Danny flicked her long, white hair back and her green eyes narrowed – not entirely with amusement. "No, Liliana I'm no mind reader but I've had a bit of experience in my day and I know that these pre-furnished flats don't come with teabags."

"Oh. Oh, I'm sorry."

"No need to be sorry dear. I'm not out to rattle you, just trying to help you. Now, supplies. At the grocery store. Need any?"

Liliana smiled then because she didn't know what else she was supposed to do. There was no doubt that this lady, her new neighbour, had rattled her. But it was strange. She didn't feel like she was someone to be avoided. What was it about these country people? They were so direct.

"Supplies. Right. Tea. Yes could you get me some

teabags...milk and bread and marg. Oh, is that too much?"

"Not at all. Be pleased to help. Pardon me if I say so Liliana, but you look like you've not had much help from anyone."

She met Danny's eyes. "Is it that obvious?" she said, handing her the crumpled $10 note that Jimbo had given her back.

Danny grabbed it, eyeing her sympathetically. "Only to the trained eyes. Happy settling in. I'll be back before dark."

And with that, the strange old woman with the green eyes left. It was only then that Liliana had a chance to orient herself to her new surroundings. The old lady...Danny, had been right about the furniture. It was pre-1960's she thought. Dark greens, beiges and yes a couple of vinyl chairs were a dead giveaway. She moved to the bedroom and was grateful to see the double bed – a luxury for her, having slept on a single bed all her adult life. The bedroom was slightly better than the lounge room, with its huge window that overlooked the leafy courtyard. If there was any doubt Liliana had left the city behind it was dispelled by that garden. And the air. It smelt clean, crisp and expansive. If air could be a colour, it would definitely be the colour of the sky in Wallanger – blue and cloudless, so different to the grey, green-less colours of Blacktown, and the grimy yellow of her apartment walls. Here, she knew she had a better chance of catching her breath and she felt the weight of her impersonality lift. She would put blue curtains on her bedroom windows, she decided.

Liliana explored the bathroom. Small but clean and there was a bath to luxuriate in under a shower head. At the Blacktown flat there had only been a shower, a small hand basin and mould. Separate toilet, she noted as she walked through, feeling increasingly lighter, like the air outside her front door. The kitchen, while furnished with a well-worn table and chairs, was clean too. She sighed, relieved. Time to unpack! She had a whole week to settle in and explore this strange country town with its even stranger characters, before she started work at the local library. She dragged the old black bag to her bedroom, thankful it would be the last time she would use it. As soon as she was unpacked, she took it outside to the garage shed at the back of the yard. Along with the old tyres and dusty wooden tools, she dumped her bag, eager to be rid of it. It too could gather dust and she'd take it as a mark of success if she never laid eyes on it again.

She had made do quite nicely in her bedroom, hanging her colourful scarves off the bed head and dangling her favourite brass chimes from the curtain rod. She had placed a photo of herself taken as a baby on the wall, and reluctantly put a photo frame of her mother on her dressing table. Her incense sticks and candle were on there too and she lit a stick – jasmine. The faint tang of incense wafted through the flat, making her feel at home. Her bed was adorned with a square crocheted blanket her grandmother had given her. Over the cream bedspread, the purple and blue blanket looked strangely in its place. An assortment of meagre possessions can sometimes add up to richness, she thought and her simple touches in the bedroom had caste an illusion of belonging. Liliana's room, she thought to herself. Mish mash, random and above all colourful. Of course, her closet was full of the black outfits she wore in public, and that was just the way she liked it. She closed her cupboards and went back to the lounge room. This would take longer, she thought and she would need her first pay check to accomplish a makeover of the dullness the old furniture projected. She sat down on the grey-green couch and thought about her mother. She hadn't done that in a long time, but immediately her mood sunk into her chest and her thoughts clouded.

Liliana remembered a mother with smooth blonde hair,

tanned skin and a square jaw. Her lips were thin and her eyes always appeared cold to her. She wondered what had made her mother like that; so empty and unfeeling. Even the way her mother dressed, lacked life. Those browns and greys, like she didn't want to let any life in...except when she was going out to meet her male friends, then she put on a bright yellow skirt and tight white blouse, and high heels. Most of those nights she didn't return home and Liliana was glad of that. Sometimes she brought her boyfriend home with her, and those were the worst nights. Liliana would shut herself in her room and cling to her pillow, trying to block out the noises from her mother's bedroom next door. Eventually, her mother just didn't come home and she got a phone call from her...from Darwin. That was probably the end of her relationship with her mother but she had been oddly relieved. It was like she was born to be alone, except for her grandmother. She had loved the old lady and she knew how hard her grandmother had tried to care for her but between the emphysema and her bad heart, her grandmother had passed away when Liliana was 10, before she had a chance to reciprocate the love her grandmother had given her. The small legacy her grandmother left Liliana meant she could live reasonably independently in the Blacktown flat, and put herself through university. Liliana was more than thankful for her blessings, all things considered.

She was roused from her thoughts by what was becoming a familiar knocking pattern at the door. The old lady...Danny, was back from the store. Liliana put the kettle on. Strange, her first day in Wallanger and already she had made more conversation with two strangers than she had had in Blacktown for 10 years. She opened the door and those intense green eyes that seemed to hold the world in their deepness stared back at her.

"I've got your tea and stuff. Got the kettle on? Got an hour or so before I have to go and I thought we'd catch up,"

Danny said.

"Yes, I'd like that," Liliana said, motioning to the vinyl chairs.

4 COUNTRY LIVING

"I come from farming people but I've been around the world," Danny said, blowing on her tea. "I'm not one for judgements but Lilly...do you mind if I call you that...Lilly I think you need to get out of those black outfits you wear. Doesn't make people comfortable, and certainly not people 'round here."

Liliana took a long sip of the English Breakfast tea Danny had bought. She was sure her groceries had cost more than the $10 she had given her, but she was not complaining. English Breakfast, bread, butter, marmalade, milk and eggs – that would make a nice breakfast for a couple of days until her last university cheque came through. And then she would have a spree because the following week she would be collecting her first real pay packet. She glanced around the lounge room.

"Needs a bit of cheering up doesn't it, like you! Now, as I was saying why do you wear all that black? Did someone die?"

Liliana smiled, a little sardonically at the old lady. She was persistent. "Yeah, me, about 10 years ago actually."

"Ah. Now I see, not letting anyone in, and not letting anything out. Such a shame Lilly, since I can see you're the type that would dance under the moonlight...given half a chance."

Liliana put her cup abruptly down. The reality of her situation that day, the train trip, the people she had encountered, this strange town and now this odd, odd lady, well it was too much in that moment.

"Oh for God's sake, who are you to tell me what you think you know about me?"

It was Danny's turn to smile. "Got ya! I made you talk and I made you angry, and that's good. You're letting something in, and letting something out and that's a whole lot better than blackness."

Liliana's jaw dropped and she went to talk but couldn't find the words. Danny smiled for both of them. "Don't worry Lilly. I'm not out to hurt you. It's just you kinda remind me of myself when I was your age. Don't normally have much to do with strangers but, hey, you're a neighbour now."

She locked onto Liliana's eyes and lowered her voice, like she had something important to tell her. "Take it easy, settle in. This town's not bad when you get to know it. Hell you might even find those walls might come down and you'll end up belonging to someone or something. Gotta go, I'm meeting the local beekeeper for a moonlight stroll, some honey and a nice drop of vodka before bed. Goodnight Lilly."

Liliana got up to see her out but that was unnecessary as Danny had gone as quickly as she had come, leaving her with plenty of thoughts on her first night in Wallanger. She yawned a deep yawn and was surprised at just how tired she felt. She knew she would sleep without the usual fitful dreams tonight – dreams of faceless attackers and her ever present fear. She had given up wondering what was at the root of her fear. It just didn't matter anymore. All the psychoanalysing in the world didn't change how she felt.

For as long as she could remember, she had dulled that fear and buried it in a place so deep she was hardly conscious that it existed any more. It was buried along with the hazy memories of her childhood and mixed with the drunken smell of her mother and her boyfriend's as they destroyed the peace of her childhood. She shook her head and looked out her window. It was just on sunset and the sky was ablaze with purple, yellow and a brilliant orange. The clouds were like layers of silky smooth sheets drawn across the sky. Bed. She thought about going there, lying on her crocheted blanket and thinking of her grandmother. She turned the lock on her new front door and checked the windows. No need to be afraid of intruders here…or her mother's drunk boyfriends. The block of flats that circled the green, leafy courtyard was uneventful. Working men and women, an old couple and a young family. She had noticed them throughout the afternoon, coming and going.

She walked into her new bedroom, lit another incense stick and took off her Doc Martins. What a day. In less than 24 hours she had left Blacktown behind, travelled inland for four hours to a small, nondescript country town and met a taxi driver with a love for the drink, and an old lady who managed to say all the things that pressed her buttons. In 24 hours she had begun a new life. She was tired, bone tired and she wanted to sleep. In the morning she would explore this town and perhaps then she might understand why she had taken the librarian's job, in the middle of nowhere and far, far from her old life.

She lay down on her bed and propped herself up on her elbows. She could see her reflection in the small mirror on the nearby dressing table. Dark circles stood out from a pale face. Her soft, golden brown eyes looked heavy; her long hair ruffled. She let her elbow drop and laid her head on the soft down of her pillow. The smell of incense drifted through her new bedroom and encased her in a warm cocoon of sleepiness. She closed her eyes against the day and let the sleep come in.

The brightness of the country sunshine woke her early and she got out of bed with surprising alacrity. Dressing quickly in her black jeans and grey shirt, she pulled her Doc Martins back on and made her way to the kitchen remembering Danny's breakfast gifts. The first thing she did was open her front door to the sunshine. She would eat with a view; it helped her not to feel alone. Later, munching her way through eggs, toast and marmalade and a steaming cup of English Breakfast tea, she thought about her day...and what she would do with it. First stop would be the real estate agent to make sure they got the bank transfer for four week's rent, and then the grocery store to build up her supplies. She looked around her lounge room – perhaps a trip to the Op shop to see if they had any fabrics or old pieces that might brighten things up. And then she would check in with the library, let them know she had arrived. The best thing would definitely be choosing a book to take home and bury herself in for the next week. She stuffed her backpack full of supplies for the day, an egg sandwich and her beanie. Although it was a hot day, she packed her coloured beanie. She didn't know why, other than it felt right on her head some days. Within minutes she was locking the front door behind her.

She had decided to walk into town. It was only a 10 minute walk anyway. No matter where you went in Wallanger, she thought, you could walk. Unlike the city with its militia of people and the glaring, sharp noises of traffic, walking into town would be pleasant. Liliana made her way down through the tree-lined streets and across the pedestrian access over the railway line. She walked by the front yards of families – some were getting ready for work; others were hurrying kids into cars. Liliana was aware that she felt different in this town. It was far more personal than the city, and there was friendliness in the faces she encountered. She walked on until she came to a park. She was beginning to think that...maybe...the fortresses she had built about herself all her life might not be needed here...well at least not all of them.

She sat to rest for a moment in the park. The big, old English trees that the pioneers had planted in their parks years ago provided a cool and pleasant shade in the present moment for Liliana. The grass underfoot, the little avenues of flower beds in full bloom and the rotunda at the centre, were all novel to Liliana. She was used to brick walls and graffiti. She sat staring at the simplistic beauty of the old park, surely the pride and joy of the small town of Wallanger. She was enjoying the shade, completely absent in the moment and did not see a young man sit down beside her. Dressed in moleskins and with the familiar 'elastic side' boots that all country folk wore, he seemed almost out of place on that park bench with the slightly Gothic Liliana. He cleared his throat. Momentarily, she felt a slight shiver of fear, but reason overtook and she found her voice.

"Err...can I help you?" she said in a smallish voice that was not without an edge that said, 'don't even think about messing with me'.

The young man spoke up, and Liliana noticed his blue eyes. Smiling and interested. What was it with these country people that so much openness in their eyes told so many stories?

"Ah, I certainly don't want to disturb you, but you looked like someone who needed a friend."

"Huh?" Liliana said, not really understanding what he was getting at.

"I...mean young girls dressed like you don't usually sit in parks by themselves without needing help. You kinda just looked like you did. I'm sorry if I intruded, but I was heading up to the railway station and I figured you might have missed your train or something."

Liliana glanced to her right and, yes, sure enough the station she had disembarked on yesterday was just up the road. She looked back at the young man and noticed his sandy brown hair and tanned skin. She didn't know what a typical farm boy was but she thought this person must be. She had seen the TV shows, and heard all the romantic myths about Australian farmers.

"Ah, if you think I'm a girl in distress who needs help from a farmer, well you'd be wrong," she said, with more than a hint of defiance in her voice.

He suddenly let out a huge laugh which caught her by surprise, throwing his head back and looking like he was thoroughly enjoying her discomfort. When he finally stopped laughing, he looked at her with a sideways glance, as if to say she was a bit more interesting than what she'd been when he had first sat down. She was just a little unnerved by his directness.

"Are you some sort of creep?" she asked, straight faced and not tempted in the slightest to let down her guard.

"No, I'm not. But I thought we established that." He stuck out his hand for her to shake. "My name's Ben Blackett. Pleased to meet you, even if you don't look real pleased to meet me."

It was only then that Liliana relaxed back into the park bench. She let down her guard, but not too much. "Liliana. Liliana Flint-Smith and I'm not going to say it's been a pleasure because I was quite pleased with my environment before you interrupted it."

"My word, you're fiery aren't you? Never mind. Flint-Smith. You're not related to the Flint-Smiths from Gundangarry. Nice spread they've got out that way and winning heaps of firsts at the Royal Easter Show for their Merino's."

She almost scoffed at him. "Hardly, I'm from Blacktown in the city. Know that?"

He smiled with what Liliana thought might be mischief in his expression. "No, never heard of it. And anyway you're here in Wallanger today. What brings you here? You're not like our usual visitor Liliana."

There was something in the way he used her name that made her want to stay in the park with him, and at the same time run as fast as she could in the opposite direction. She had met plenty of boys like him at university, from the surrounding highland regions, lush, rich country beyond the city's parameters. In one long moment, she decided to stay in the park and talk with him.

"I arrived here yesterday and I'm living here, actually. I start as Wallanger's junior librarian next week. I'm on my way to get a few groceries, take a look around the place and generally orient myself. I *was* enjoying the park before you showed up."

"Umm. Disturbing," he said.

"What?" she asked.

"Sorry. I mean I hope I didn't disturb you. Know what that's like myself. When I'm on the farm and...you know...lost in a sunset, well I don't like to be disturbed. Sorry. Sorry if I disturbed you."

She relaxed. "No problems, but I really must go." She got up to leave, not before noticing his sky blue shirt matched his eyes.

"Oh. Yeah sure," he said, with just a hint of disappointment, she noted mentally. "Hope to see you around sometime then. I'll just be heading up to the station now. Was picking my grandmother up from the train and had to duck down to the shops for a minute. But I'm glad I came this way Liliana Flint-Smith of Blacktown."

She half thought he might have been mocking her, but his face was serious and, Liliana thought, sincere.

"Look...Ben..."

He interrupted. "Now don't say we won't see each other again, because I forgot to tell you that I read a lot of novels and we'll catch up in the library."

"Really, you're a bookworm? I wouldn't have guessed." She began to get drawn into another conversation and stopped her impulse. "But, really, I've got to go. See you."

"Yeah. See you Liliana."

She hurried away as quickly as her Doc Martins would carry her, not wanting to appear foolish. It was only when she got far enough down the road that she let out a huge sigh of relief. What was it with this town? Surely they could see she wasn't like them. Surely they should leave her alone. She imagined how she looked to them. When she got to the main street, she searched for someone else dressed like her. There was, quite simply, no-one. No arguments, not one single person was dressed remotely like her. She must stick out like a cactus in a meadow. That's what she was, a prickly cactus.

Never mind. She never expected to belong here in Wallanger just because she was starting a new life away from the grime and dirt and greyness of the city. And she simply loved her new flat, and even the thought of that strange old woman next door was a bit comforting. Yep, all and all she thought, as she pushed open the door to the small supermarket and started mentally thinking about a grocery list, things could be worse and she knew from experience they were a whole lot better than Blacktown.

That thought put a spring in her step and she glanced down the aisles of food before pausing at the dairy section and the gourmet cheeses. Yes the Swiss cheddar looked good. Umm, maybe cheese, biscuits and a small bottle of wine might be in order tonight…to watch the purple/orange swirl of a Wallanger sunset. Immediately, she thought of Ben Blackett.

5 MAKING A HOME

Liliana spent the week making her flat into a home. It was the first time a place really belonged to her; not like the Blacktown flat which really belonged to her mum. No, this place was clean - and fresh and sunny - and with a few of her touches it was full of those cosy corners and comfortable spaces to sit, lie or stretch out, away from the world. This home was her first haven.

She enjoyed shopping for oddments at the local Op shop. She had found a brass lamp base with a gingham shade and a couple of brass ornaments to match – a man igniting a lamplight with a large lighting stick, and a woman walking her dogs. Both scenes were intricate and she marvelled at how someone could create them in brass. A few colourful throw rugs brightened the dull green lounge, and she found her biggest treasure of all, a large bookshelf which now occupied half the lounge room wall. Thanks to Jimbo and the boot of his taxi, it now occupied pride of place. Into the bookshelf she put the few books she was able to carry in her big black bag and a few she had bought at the Op shop. She filled some of the spaces with little glass ornaments she had also found and she put her huge purple amethyst crystal on top of the bookcase. Just the bookcase and a few little touches and the atmosphere had completely changed.

She also loved the kitchen, which she brightened with fresh flowers from the garden in the assortment of old vases she had found under the sink. Anybody walking into her flat would be greeted with the sweet smell of roses and rhododendrons which spread their colour across Liliana's rooms, and her life. She marvelled in the freedom that Wallanger had given her and she began to grow to love her newfound domesticity. In Blacktown, her flat was simply a place to exist within, away from the glare and impersonality of the city. Its darkness and mustiness almost made her sick but it was better than nothing and better than she had ever known.

Danny came and went during the week with almost alarming frequency. Just when Liliana was beginning to think her new acquaintance was too neighbourly, Danny would sprout some wisdom which gave Liliana comfort and, in an odd kind of way, support.

"You know, I think you are going through a transition stage in your life," she would say, randomly, almost as if she was speaking to herself.

"A transition," Liliana scoffed. "If transition is a semi-hard time that you have to do alone, then maybe. And if it's that, then I've been going through a transition for most of my life. In fact, the last time I wasn't going through a transition was when I was being breastfed for the six weeks before my mother thought it was about time she started drinking again. Transitions. Hmmph."

But Danny persisted. "Well may be so, but real transitions are about finding your way in the half light and learning how well you can see. You might have been knocking around in the dark before Liliana, but I'm not sure you weren't bumping into the furniture of life. Now, I think you're beginning to see."

Liliana could only shake her head. She wasn't beginning to 'see' at all. Aside from her flat, she didn't think she belonged in this town. There was no-one else like her here – the young girls were sun-browned barbie dolls; the blokes were boot scootin cowboys and the old people she had met so far were, well, a bit strange.

"Ok Danny, how'd you end up in Wallanger?"

"Good question Liliana. I moved here from the city when I was about your age but I was raised on a farm in the beginning. It wasn't exciting enough for me, so I moved to the city and got married. When I came to Wallanger, back to the country again, I'd just come off a bad, bad marriage. He was the possessive type and had been hitting me. Didn't like it when I got any power at all. I got a promotion at work and it meant I had to attend networking functions and stay back a bit. I was quite proud of myself, and excited too because I had goals and ambitions, and it was the start of our lives together. I thought I could make something for myself and for him too. But that wasn't quite what my husband wanted for me. He saw me as an extension of himself and my role was definitely to make him look better, not to have any kind of success for myself. Sounds harsh, but that's the way he was. I don't even think he was a bad man, just a misguided one. Anyway, after the third beating, I wasn't hanging around for a fourth. I am not one of those women who can take that – being a punching bag - so I packed my bags, quit my job and headed south. Ended up here and made a good life for myself."

Liliana looked at her thoughtfully, and in a new light. She knew a woman like Danny, with those penetrating green eyes, had been around. It made sense. "And what did you do once you got here?"

"Oh, found myself a place to live. Got a job as a junior in the office and worked my way up. Had a good career and made some good friends. Learned to paint too, and I'm well regarded as a landscape artist round these parts – bet that was something you didn't know 'bout me…"

"And fell in love?" Liliana said, not really knowing why she had said that.

Danny looked out her window, to the horizon beyond, her green eyes focused on her life's possibilities and realities. "No...no I never married again, or fell in love again. Sometimes you have to give up what you love and there's no liking it, but it has to be done and got through. I gave up on love when I packed my bags that day and left my husband."

"Oh," Liliana said, as if realising that there was no more to be said.

Slowly, she began to look forward to Danny's visits. And Jimbo the taxi driver was also busying himself driving her to and from the main street and helping her with the bits and pieces she was starting to accumulate. Between the two of them, the first few weeks in Wallanger were made less lonely and infinitely more meaningful than a lifetime in Blacktown. As she walked to work that first day, past the families getting ready to start their morning, past the leafy green park and railway station and down along the quiet, country lanes of the town, she was struck by the simplicity of living. Rather than people and things crowding out the space inside her in the city, the country's vastness seemed to extend her. In the country, Liliana was able to reach in and find her soul, that part of her that was indescribable but so tangibly around her, and as real as the green trees and blue sky that occupied so much of the space she lived in now.

She didn't want to admit it but something about the country gave her freedom in a way the anonymity of the city never did. It didn't really matter to her that nobody dressed like her, and that all the young people her age didn't remotely resemble her. What mattered was that here she was beginning to know who she was, and what she wanted for herself. In a way, it was all about how much ground she gave up to the world, and how much she kept for herself. It was with this attitude that Liliana approached her first day at work.

She had done a reconnaissance on the library the week before, walking round the big, old brick building that was attached to the town's council chambers. She had read it had been built in the 1800's not long after the town was established by a farming family that pushed on past the last frontier town, to an old telegraph outpost. There they discovered the fertile plains so characteristic of the Wallanger country. The early settlers had put a value on books and reading. Back in those days, books were sought after and separated the civilised from the supposed 'uncivilised', she thought. Liliana thought that meant that books broadened your horizon and gave you the opportunity to listen to what a variety of people had to say. She had never subscribed to the theory that books 'educated'. No, books could open up vistas that may not have been contemplated before.

Arriving on her first day Liliana pushed open the heavy, oak door that framed an archway to the front section of the library and looked around her new workplace. Like the council chamber, the library was a grand building with ornamental windows and stonework that gave it a hint of power, setting it apart from the other buildings in the street. She noticed a young girl on the counter. She was dressed like the other country girls, blue shirt and brown pants, pink lipstick and her hair in a ponytail. But Liliana stopped herself from making any further snap judgements. She didn't want to do the very thing people had done to her. Approaching the counter, she smiled openly at the girl. She had dressed in a black trouser suit and white shirt and she felt business-like and competent on her first day.

"Hi, I'm Liliana Flint-Smith," she said to the girl. "I'm starting here today at the library…as a librarian."

The young girl in the blue shirt smiled a warm, friendly smile. "I know, Melody said you'd be arriving today. She's gone over to our sister library in Beaufort today for training, but she'll be back tomorrow. She said you should settle in and find your way round the place. We've got a desk for you, out the back here. Oh…I'm

Julie…Julie Taylor."

Liliana came round the counter. "Pleased to meet you Julie, and thanks."

She followed Julie into the office behind the reception to one of three desks in the spacious room. She could hardly contain the smile when Julie showed her to the desk by a big arched window. It had a view across the main street.

"Will you be right here…there's your computer and passwords too," she said pointing to a note on her desk from Melody with a list of instructions for the day. "I think Melody wanted you to follow up a few inter-library loans, and there'll be the usual things, attending to borrower requests, answering the emails…but Melody said this was to be a day for you to 'find yourself in the library', whatever that means. I have to get back to reception now; I think that was the front door."

Liliana thanked her. The day was starting well, and she liked the informality.

She watched as Julie's ponytail swished through the door and back to reception. She sat down and oriented herself. Outside, the country street was beginning to come to life. A girl carrying four coffees walked by, crossed the road and went into the clothes shop. She was dressed in a soft pink, tight dress and high heels. Her blond hair cascaded in long waves down her back. She was no older than Liliana. A couple of business men in suits, deep in conversation passed by the window. Slightly balding and with that country swagger that looked awkward in the city. A few teenagers dressed in short school uniforms with heavy eye makeup headed around the corner, presumably walking to school. Liliana knew it wouldn't be long before she knew all these characters, and they would know her – a rather uncomfortable thought.

She looked around the room. It was what she expected from a library office. Trays of books, lots of paper, but orderly at the same time. She noticed the posters on the wall. One was from the Great Gatsby movie, the other from the Book Thief. She smiled to herself, and immediately felt at home. These two titles were amongst her favourite books, but then coincidences generally happen when you least expect it, she thought.

She turned her computer on and glanced down the list of inter-library loans she needed to get through. She noticed Ben Blackett's name on the list. Coincidence? She thought so, given the loan request was made two weeks ago before they met in the park. She searched the form to discover what book he'd ordered. Ben Blackett had ordered her favourite book, about a world without books and the resultant anarchy. Words were life; words were one of the things that kept the concept of peace and love alive. She processed his order, and put his name on the list of those for Julie to contact. His book would be in on Wednesday, two days away.

She finished working through the list of loans and checked her emails. There was a 'welcome' from Wallanger Council, as she was technically employed by them. Nice to be welcomed, she thought and she made a mental note that her employer had at least ticked one box; and a bright and cheery hello from her boss, Melody. Next was a tour of the library, she took a trolley of books with her to put away and once that was done she explored the aisles of fiction and non-fiction. It didn't matter how many books she saw, the spines, the titles and the words inside were treasures to be preserved she thought. Imagine a world without books; she quite simply couldn't. Before she knew it, the day had whizzed by. She had spent some time with Julie over a cup of tea at lunch time, and concluded she really was quite sweet.

When she walked out that evening Jimbo was waiting for her. "Thought you might need a lift home Liliana, and I was in the neighbourhood."

She nodded, not game to protest that he might be just being a bit too insistent on looking out for her, because he looked like he'd been up all night.

"You alright Jimbo? You haven't been drinking again?"

He closed his eyes as if trying to block out the world, she thought. "Might have been. It's not a crime, and I would know. The alcohol's long left my system."

She laughed. "Yes I suppose you would. Come on let's get going. I've got some nice plunger coffee."

He went to thank her, but she cut in "I know Jimbo. Shut up and drive."

It was a few hours before she was able to get Jimbo out her door. She ended up cooking him a meal and giving him multiple cups of coffee. The reason for his relapse? Yesterday he had heard from his daughter who was living in Sydney with her mum, Jimbo's ex wife. He hadn't heard from the girl in five years, not since his ex wife had walked out the door with their three children. His daughter wanted to come and see him. Liliana supposed the shock of it had driven Jimbo to the bottle and a bender. He was well and truly sober now, but he had more of that sunken look around his eyes. Defeated and deflated, like her mum used to look. By the time he left Liliana was yawning and ready for bed. Tomorrow she would meet Melody, and Ben Beckett would be in to pick up his book; her book, the book he had ordered before he met her. She hopped into bed and thought about coincidence again. Were some meetings destined to occur? Had she been brought to Wallanger for a purpose, and if so why? She felt like she had known the people around her for a lifetime – Jimbo, Danny, even Julie in a funny kind of way. And then there was Ben, a random meeting in a park and now he would be back in the library, her library.

She opened her blinds on the full moon and its light shone brightly in her room. If she hadn't been so tired she would have got up and danced under it, butt naked, just for the hell of it. Instead she drifted off to sleep with a vague thought about what she was going to say to Ben Blackett when he walked through the big old archway door of the library.

6 NEW DAY, NEW JOB

The sun coming through Liliana's windows woke her before the alarm clock had a chance to brutally interrupt sleep. Instead, she stretched lazily and let the warm rays fall uninterrupted onto her cheeks. She drifted between that place of sleep and wakefulness; that lazy, pleasant feeling that permeates the body right to the finger tips was spreading through her and she drifted back, deeper into sleep. Images of faces and places came to mind, like a kaleidoscope of her life. The grey/black streets of the city, overcast skies and the feeling of always being on the outside came to her. Her mother, with her bruised and beaten face and her false happiness at the end of a bottle, the un-realness of her university days and trains. Tracks leading to an alternative destination, but Liliana couldn't see what lay ahead. She squirmed in her sleep, and the pleasant feelings began to leave her. Somewhere in the back of her mind, she knew she had to get up for work. She dragged herself out of bed and into the shower.

Forty minutes later, she closed her door and began the walk into town. She half thought about calling Jimbo on her mobile for a free lift, but she thought a walk might clear her head. The half dreams of the morning had unnerved her. Perhaps it was a delayed reaction to all that had happened to her in the short time she'd been in Wallanger. One part of her thought about the anonymity the city provided. At least catching the 301 bus to university hadn't unnerved her like the way she felt this morning. As she headed towards the library, she half thought about diverting to the train station and hopping onboard a train to Sydney. What was it about getting to know people that prickled her skin and rattled her senses, she thought. Far easier to be alone in a crowd. Instead she walked through Wallanger Library's archway doors and saw a new face at reception. This time the woman was middle aged, with a soft face and intelligent eyes. This must be Melody, Liliana thought.

"Hi...hello, I'm Liliana," she said rather timidly.

The woman looked up from her work and gave Liliana a half smile – she wasn't one for exuberance Liliana noted. "Liliana, I'm Melody. Melody Thomas. Welcome to Wallanger Library."

Liliana smiled a half smile back. "Thanks, you have a lovely library."

"Really?" Melody said, indicating she should sit down on the nearby couch. The library at this hour was quiet. One person was sitting at its far end, on the armchair beside the arched window reading. "I suppose I don't look at it with a newcomer's eyes. It is what we created and if that is inspiration and that feeling of contentedness that you get when you read a book, then we have created space for that here."

Liliana nodded. She was beginning to warm to Melody Thomas – another in Wallanger that seemed to understand her. "I couldn't agree more. I've always felt that way about books, and the need to preserve them for society. There is something about taking a book between your hands and reading its pages. It's almost as if you are sitting with its author; existing in the same thought stream almost...but I'm starting to ramble now..."

"Not at all Liliana. I love books as much as you do, and I chose you above 80 candidates for this job because I knew that was how you felt about books. We are, in a way, custodians of books and heaven help us if there comes a day when books are not as valued, or appreciated for all the gifts they have to give us. But there is the internet…"

Liliana shifted in her seat. She was an avid e-book reader. "Oh, you mean e-books?"

"No, not necessarily. I mean there is so much information available now online, that we are in danger of being overloaded and not reading books. I mean look at the rise of 'posting' quotations. Are we going to get our fix from those? It's a bit Orwellian don't you think?"

Liliana glanced around at the library which was starting to fill now. "Orwellian? Umm, maybe but I think as long as there are people like us to preserve the books, then fads finish and people always look back and discover what was real, and what was of value. It will be like that with books, particularly hard covers. They will be sought out in the future, I'm sure."

Melody smiled, only this time her eyes were happy. "You are an optimist aren't you, and I'm sorry to have had this intense chat on your first morning. It's just that I love it when I meet another book lover. Now, down to business. I would like you to begin cataloguing the children's book section of the library. How does that sound?"

"Perfectly fine to me. I must say that I am not as familiar with children's books as I am with adult literature but it will be a learning experience. I just didn't get that exposure when I was a child myself."

Melody nodded. "Perfectly understandable. Not everyone is raised by Walt Disney you know. It's ok. In any case, you may just discover your inner child."

With that, she got up and began to greet a customer, leaving Liliana to ponder the strange conversation with her new boss. Children's books…ugh Liliana thought. She didn't like to admit it to Melody but she was not enthused by the prospect of wading through Dr Zuess, or even the famously famous Harry Potter series. She knew magical childhoods were mostly a myth; and that childhood was and is difficult for many adults and children. Bad things happened to children who were the most vulnerable people on the planet aside from the very elderly, she thought. But it was a job that needed doing, and she would do it for Melody who, after all, had taken a punt, hiring her from 80 candidates and bringing her all the way from Sydney to Wallanger to begin work. She may be sullen, quiet and rude to most people, most of the time, but she knew that loyalty was amongst her best qualities. She would return the favour to Melody tenfold because in her life favours were a rarity.

She put her bag down at her desk and checked her emails. Ah ha! Ben Blackett's book had arrived. She located it in the morning's mail and put it under the front counter at reception, with strict instructions for Julie to give it to him if he came in today to pick it up. She really didn't want to see him again and, if she could, she would avoid it. Avoidance had kept her safe for years and she wasn't going to start changing these habits quickly.

The day drifted on and Liliana immersed herself in the children's section of the library. It wasn't until Julie tapped her shoulder at lunch time to tell her she was needed at reception, that she realised where she was, lost as she was in the catalogue of fantasy adventures. She assumed Julie wanted her to relieve at reception, so she followed without question. As she approached the desk, she saw the familiar silhouette of Ben Blackett – the light brown, wavy hair flicked back by hand to follow a natural curl, the confident pose and Roman like profile that said he hadn't suffered a day in his charmed life. She almost stopped on the spot as she searched for potential escape routes. She kept seeing the green Exit signs above the doors and momentarily contemplated walking towards them, out the door and back to the train station. She hadn't bargained on complications in Wallanger – the kind of complications that hit at the heart and penetrated her numbness. Instead, she kept walking and forced a smile.

"Ben isn't it?" she said as she approached, finding her voice from somewhere.

He turned to face her and she was immediately struck by his blue eyes, again. "Yeah, Liliana. Liliana Flint-Smith." His voice was low and smooth, and reminded her of a young cowboy out of the movies. It had a particular charm for her ears, and she felt herself blushing.

"Err…I have your book," she ventured.

He shifted, leaning his elbow on the front counter and not taking his eyes off her for a second. She could feel the air begin to almost crackle around her and she was in danger of falling into those blue and strangely familiar eyes. She caught herself in time and found her voice again.

"Well if that's all Ben, I'll be getting back to my work." She turned to go.

He straightened up and took a step towards her, as if sensing she was about to flee back behind the rows of bookshelves. "Well actually that's not all. I want you to come for lunch with me and I'm not taking no for an answer."

She backed away from him, surprised by his intensity. She wasn't used to this up close and personal experience with anyone, let alone a man and she hated the way it made her feel. Far better to be have no feeling, than a feeling that was frightening, unfamiliar and unwanted.

"I don't think so Ben…I'll be working through lunch."

The immediate look of disappointment on his face changed her mind. "But maybe a quick one?" Strangely, she didn't want to hurt him in any way.

His face brightened. "Thanks. I just want to talk about the book with you. I know you'll understand. Where I come from they think I'm a poofter or something because I read books. They wonder why I'm not out in the paddock shooting rabbits." He leant closer to her. "The truth is I'm a vegetarian and love nothing better than to cook up a mushroom risotto or chilli tofu…"

Liliana almost let out a roar of laughter. His confession was the last thing she expected. She half wondered if he was joking, but the look on his face told her he wasn't.

"I'm sorry Ben. I didn't know…just assumed you were the boot scootin' cowboy type and, for some reason, trying to make a joke out of me."

He touched her arm with the lightest and most unobtrusive of gestures. "No Liliana, simply gravitating to a like-minded friend. I don't want to scare you off though and if you'd rather not come, I'll understand."

She adopted her most business-like of tones to assure him she was committed to lunch with him. "No, I'd love to go. Where would you like to eat?"

"Sally's Corner. It's got good lentil burgers there. Oh, and plenty of fish, chicken and red meat for you as well."
She smiled at him, almost getting lost in those eyes again. "Brilliant, I'll see you there. One-ish?"

"Perfect," he said in his low cowboy drawl. "I'll see ya then."

She turned back to the rows of shelves completely lost in her thoughts about Ben Blackett. She began her cataloguing again; she had reached 'E' and had already immersed herself in fairies, tree spirits and leprechauns, but when she got to 'D', all she could think about was Ben's confession. Who would have thought that he was as lost and out of place as she was – and as alone too, more than likely?"

She picked up a story book about a little puppy who thought he was a sheep. He ate, slept and played with the sheep, but his brothers and sisters turned on him. It was only through his dad deciding to stand by his son that the little puppy was free to be himself. She wondered what support Ben Blackett was getting from his family at home on the farm. If he was reaching out to her – another person who knew what it was like not to belong – then she imagined he wasn't receiving much support at all. But she had had no-one to support her either. Momentarily, she was caught by the view through the nearby archway window. The street outside was full of activity, people of all ages, busying themselves with whatever was occupying their minds at that time. She wondered how many felt like they didn't belong where they were, and what would it take for them to find their place, their belonging place.

Her thoughts were interrupted by Julie approaching. "Liliana I'm back from lunch now. Do you want to take yours?"

She glanced at her watch. It was 12.45pm. "Yes, thanks Julie."

It wasn't long before she was walking through the front door of Sally's Corner. Her gaze locked onto Ben's in the crowd as she made her way over to the table. It was a corner table, under the window and relatively private.

"Hi, I'm glad you could make it," he said. She sat down, not knowing what to do next.

"Listen before we start with the small talk, I've got something I needed to get off my chest with you," he said, silencing anything further she might attempt to do to start the conversation.

"With me. I don't think so. I hardly even know you," she said.

"But I know you…well at least I feel I know you," he replied. "I saw you leave the train station that day at precisely the same time I was going to catch the train out of Wallanger. There you were with that big, black bag and that coloured beanie pulled down over your face as far as it could go. Yeah, I noticed you weren't like the other girls in the town, but something in the way you walked, and in the way you came to Wallanger by yourself, gave me the hope, I suppose, that I could be myself. There. I've said it, and got it off my chest…I just wanted you to know…in case you thought I was some creep obsessed with you. Well I am, really. I want to get to know you Liliana."

Her almond eyes widened and she felt her cheeks blush. Never, ever, had she been singled out for attention. Usually, she blended into the background. It seemed coming to Wallanger had made her noticeable and she wasn't sure how she felt about that. "I'm flattered but I'm nothing special Ben. You're wrong about me. I'm no guiding light for your battered and bruised identity." And then, because she wanted to distance herself from him. "And because the silver spoon doesn't fit into your country mouth."

She waited for him to respond, hardly daring to look at him. She had surprised herself with her prickliness but she was used to being alone and not having to share herself with anyone. For one long moment he was silent before the smile began on his face, widening with every shake of his head.

"No doubt about you Liliana *Flint*-Smith, you surely know how to put someone in their place don't you?"

She reached for the menu. "I'm not trying to do that; just want to make the boundaries clear ok? Ready to order?" she said, smiling as she said it, pleased she had, seemingly, got the upper hand.

He smiled back at her, understanding her motives and happy to know her despite her standoffishness. "I am, and there's something else. I want you to come walking with me on Friday night out on the farm. I want to show you the other reason why I didn't get on that train that night."

She thought briefly about it. "Sure, if I can bring my sketch pad. I'm a 'drawer' as well as a reader."

He smiled at that. "As long as I can show you some of my writing. I'd be interested to hear what you think."

And so, at Sally's Corner in Wallanger at precisely 1.10pm on a Tuesday in summer, she dropped her guard in front of a man for the first time in her life.

7 BREAKING DOWN WALLS

All week Liliana paced: in her flat from end to end, up and down the library corridors during her breaks, and criss-crossed as much of Wallanger that anyone could in a week. There were streets and lanes not even some of the locals had heard of that she walked. As soon as she finished work she would rush home, scoff some food and get changed into her trackpants and sneakers. She was a girl possessed. Even Danny couldn't reach her. Liliana walked, as if coming to some conclusion invisible to those surrounding her. A silent, sacred transition, deep, lasting and life changing.

She thought about her life and her mother. She thought about the long, lonely years and the walls she had constructed around herself to keep others out. Already they were crumbling down around her and she didn't know what to do. She went over her motives for coming to Wallanger and she imagined futures for herself. She thought about Ben Beckett, and the friends she was beginning to make at the library. She thought of Danny and Jimbo, lost souls like her who had found a sense of belonging in Wallanger. Broken souls, torn by hurt and tragedy, and the cracks still visible.

Liliana tried to pinpoint her own soul and capture the essence of who she was, as if that was the answer, but it was like trying to catch vapour in a jar. She didn't know who she would become which meant she didn't really know herself…yet.

She understood that she had found more 'belonging' in Wallanger than ever before, certainly more than in Blacktown, but she also knew that wasn't the whole solution. In Ben she could lose herself, and he in her, two random souls meeting at a time of similar need. She drifted into that thought, but her feet kept walking, pacing to and fro, like a pendulum swinging with time.

The days went by until Friday dawned. The day she had committed to that evening walk with Ben. She got through her day as best she could, fobbing off the worried looks from Melody and Julie. She didn't know what was wrong, only that something was. Ben had arranged to come and pick her up from her flat and as she hurried home that afternoon, she took out her mobile phone ready to…what? Ring him and cancel, she thought. As if that would be a solution. Instead she threw on a vintage white dress with large rose swirls. She pulled her doc martins on, reluctant to dispense with them. They were, after all, her security blanket. But the dress, the slight tan the Wallanger sun had given her, her long brown hair minus the beanie – this was a Liliana few had seen.

Danny came knocking, perhaps sensing Liliana's makeover and drew in her breath. "Oh my God Liliana, you are beautiful! Where are you going dressed like that?"

Liliana rolled her eyes. "Danny don't make a fuss. I'm merely going out to Ben Blackett's farm for an evening walk."

Danny laughed. "Well let's hope he doesn't ask you to help with the muster…dressed like that."

"What. What's wrong with my dress?" She began to unbutton the back.

"No. Don't do that. I'm joking Liliana. Joking, you know, making light of things, getting into this exciting prospect you have presented me with. What is it with Ben Blackett and you? You know he's from one of the oldest farming families in this district. There would be other girls in Wallanger extremely jealous of you tonight."

"Stop it Danny. It's not like that. Really, it's not. He's just…well going through some soul searching, like me and we are kind of ships passing in the night. It's not serious. He just wants to talk that's all – to someone he thinks understands him."

Danny helped herself to one of Liliana's apples. "Umm. And what do you think Liliana. What if it's more than that?"

"It can't be," she said staring at the orange and purple swirl in the afternoon sky. "It's not my belonging place…"

Danny frowned. "Belonging place…what on earth are you talking about?"

"Nothing…nothing. It's nothing…" At that moment, Ben's Ford ute pulled up. She hurried out to meeting him. "Lock up will you Danny."

She half ran down the driveway to greet Ben. She had almost come to a decision. Almost glimpsed into her future self. Almost had the courage of her convictions. Almost. Ben was pleased to see her, his blue eyes reflecting the huge grin on his face. "Liliana, you're just beautiful."

She lowered her eyes. "No, not really."

"Yes, really. Now get in or we'll miss this brilliant sunset."

She was mostly silent on the way out to Ben's farm. Past the straw coloured fields; past the green woody patches in between. Everywhere animals grazed obliviously on fertile pastures, living in the moment. Liliana knew most would go to the slaughterhouse. It wasn't something she liked to dwell on. No wonder Ben was a vegetarian. Well-read and sensitive, he can't have liked the thought that he was raising living things to take to their death.

Before long, they were turning into his farm and heading toward the back paddocks. "There's something I want to show you," he said, shifting into low gear for the rocky path they were on.

"Where are you taking me?" she said, with just a hint of concern. After all, she didn't know that much about Ben Blackett. What if he couldn't be trusted?" She had a moment of panic and was about to ask him to take her home but she fought it down. She understood that this was a moment of importance, for Ben and for herself.

They pulled up at what could only be described as an oasis. Thick wooded trees hid a small creek that ran through the centre of the forest. The green grass was lush and cool against the summer evening's air. He opened the door for her.

"Thank you for this, Liliana. It's my special place, made all the more special because of you."

She got out and walked to the edge of the oasis. "No, it's me that needs to thank you Ben."

He looked at her with intensity and she felt herself drawn into the blueness again. "You don't need to thank me Liliana. By some miracle you've entered my life, at a time when I doubted everything – when I was about to run away. You've given me the courage to stay."

She walked over to the nearby fallen tree, a makeshift seat on the grassy blanket, and sat down, in full view of the sunset and its brilliance. He sat down beside her.

They began talking simultaneously: "I want to talk to you…" And then they smiled. "You first," she said, trying to still the churn in the pit of her stomach.

"Ok, here goes. I wanted you here tonight to share with you what's so special in my life. You know that before I met you, was inspired by you, I was ready to catch the train out of here. I've never felt at home. I'm just not like my brothers – more like my mum who is a poet. I never felt I belonged here. You must know that feeling…anyway, you turned up and because of one random meeting I stayed. I want to get to know you more Liliana."

He leant over and she became lost again in his eyes – blues merged with purples and oranges and she could have been forgiven for thinking that destiny had had the last laugh. Their lips locked and she felt new and unaccustomed warmth in her body. But she pulled back, gently pushing him away.

"Ben...Ben, I can't..."

He looked hurt and straightened up, puzzled. "I thought you wanted this?"

She was just as confused, but held onto her earlier decision. "I do, I do. Just let me finish, please."

"Sorry Liliana. I'm sorry. What do you need to say to me?"

She swallowed hard. This was more difficult than she had anticipated.

"Well firstly Ben, I want to thank you. You, out of everyone I've met in Wallanger, have made me feel strong in myself, and in a short time I've learned from you. You were right. We didn't meet by chance. I believe two people are attracted to one another at the very time they need to be, when they both want the same thing and when the time is right for them to meet. I don't believe in coincidences Ben."

"No, neither do I Liliana."

She continued, half ignoring him and intent on saying what she needed to say. "...I believe I met you for a reason Ben, and that was to find our belonging places. You had already realised yours wasn't here and you were on the way to the station when you met me, a girl who thumbed her nose at what other people thought she should be. A girl who didn't belong."

He reached for her hand. "That's right Liliana..."

"...And a boy who didn't belong. But Ben I've found that Wallanger is helping me to belong. I don't know if it's my belonging place but it's a hell of a good start so far. For the first time in a lifetime, I actually want to talk to people. I don't feel the need to put up huge, fortress defences. I trust the people I meet, and let me tell you, that's huge for me. You have no idea. And then there is you Ben. I would love; I mean like to get to know you better. You have to believe me when I say that but...I, well, I..."

His grip on her hand tightened. "Say it Liliana...just say it."

"I believe in my heart you should have got on that train, and to stay in Wallanger when you don't feel you belong is a mistake. It's a mistake Ben you'll regret. It's a mistake that's going to hold you back in the future. Oh yeah, how easy would it be...you and me. We could keep each other satisfied learning about each other, opening the doors to different lives. It would be fun and exciting...for a while. But is it enough? Do we find our belonging place in each other?"

He pulled her closer to him. "I don't care Liliana; I think it would be enough."

"No. No," she said, with more force the second time. "It wouldn't and you know it Ben Blackett. You know deep down inside that your belonging place is within you. Not in me. Not in this farm. It's in you." She put her hand on his heart and looked deeply within his eyes.

"Go away Ben. Go away and find your belonging place."

His eyes were ablaze with the sunset, with the cool greenness of the oasis and with his understanding of her. He bowed his head. She wiped away the tear that began to slide down her cheek.

"I know Liliana. As much as I don't want to hear it. I know. And you know what?"

"What?" she said, wiping the salty tear track on her face.

"I don't want to stop you belonging here. And I don't want to stop you doing what it is you're meant to be doing. Promise me one thing."

She sniffled, "Anything. Anything."

"I want you to promise me you will come here and

draw my sunset for me…and send it to me…where-ever I may be."

She leant into him then, and he to her. The sky overhead deepened and the dusk fell. They didn't move and, in that moment, the sunset spread its rays outward, touching two young people at the start of their lives. It brought with it a promise of belonging.

BOOK 2

ESTELLE'S STORY

1 AN EARLY START

She flicked the cappuccino machine on as she whizzed through the kitchen, brush in one hand, daycare lunch in the other. A quick, furtive glance at the kitchen clock told her she had exactly 10 minutes to get Corey ready for daycare. "Joel, Joel, we've got to go! Can you hurry…please!" she yelled up the stairwell. By some miracle he would've heard and would miraculously appear down the stairs, on time. She knew he wouldn't be doing that, so she called again, louder this time. "Joel, Joel. Come on!"

She grabbed a piece of toast out of the toaster and smeared it with vegemite. Corey was getting fidgety in his high chair. She smiled at him, as she grabbed his coat and hat from the table. "Coming my little man. Just give mummy one more minute. Joel, I'm not kidding…"

She was about to tell her husband what she really thought about his lateness but he appeared round the corner while she was in mid-sentence. His blonde hair untidy, but in a suit and with his briefcase in his hands, nevertheless. "In the nick of time, by the looks of things," he said, planting a quick kiss on her cheek as he walked past, eager to get to the cappuccino machine. Two cappuccinos coming up," he said, getting the stainless steel flasks out of the cupboard.

"You are a lifesaver," she said, unstrapping her young son from his highchair. He was the image of his blonde haired, blue eyed dad. "There you go baby. Mummy's just about ready." She kissed his round, still baby cheeks and ran the brush lightly through his hair. "Now, let's get your coat on. It's brrrr outside and I don't want you getting cold." Her son looked up at her with his big blue eyes, a big smile on his face. She could have said anything to him, she thought, and he would still be smiling up at her. A pang of guilt shot through her. Why was she dragging her toddler out the door on such a cold winter's day? She shook her head. "Now let's not go through all that again Estelle," she said to herself.

"What darling? What did you say?" Joel said, grabbing her coat for her.

"Nothing. Talking to myself. Going mad actually; must be this new job promotion."

He took Corey from her and pointed to the freshly brewed cappuccinos in their steel flasks. "You take these darling and I'll go and strap munchkins in his car seat. Oh, and Estelle don't forget your briefcase like yesterday."

She looked at him as if to say 'are you questioning my memory'. "Ok Joel, yes I forgot it yesterday, but we were in such a rush..."

"Like today," he countered. "And I'm only trying to help."

She waved him out the door and did a last minute check of the kitchen to make sure everything was turned off. She picked up her half eaten vegemite toast, the baby bag for Corey and her briefcase. One last hurried look in the mirror, and a mental note to get her long black hair cut on the weekend into a more manageable, shorter style, and she was out the door.

Getting into the car with her son and husband, she heaved a huge sigh of relief. "Made it."

He smiled at her and flicked the car into gear. "God, the day has only just begun and I'm exhausted," he said with a grin on his face.

She smiled, a half-hearted attempt at agreement, and fell silent. Corey dozed in the back. She had been up half the night with him. He had come home from daycare with the snuffles, a head cold picked up from one of the other 50 children there. Another pang of guilt. Stop it, she told herself. Just stop it. She leant her head back on the plush leather headrest of their Audi. Money had not been a problem for them for the past two years. Before, she was struggling to make it up the ladder in the editorial room, and Joel hadn't been promoted to senior architect. Since then they'd both received promotions, she to Editor of the Woman's Post and he to senior partner in Bladwell & Sons Architects. They had upgraded their home to a posh part of the city, and along with the move, bought the Audi. To anyone who noticed these things, they were a highly successful couple, with a beautiful baby boy. They had, quite simply, everything…and nothing she thought. She craved a day at home and reasoned that must be why she couldn't lift herself out of her current downer. She was just tired and nearing the end of her patience with the breakneck pace of her life, and its impacts on her family. Time for a holiday perhaps?

She gazed at the blur of suburban Sydney as it whirred past the tinted glass of the Audi's windows. They lived on the North Shore now and it was a longer drive into the City. She had found a good daycare centre a few suburbs along and they were approaching it. She called softly to her son. "Honey, we're nearly at daycare. Nearly time to see Benny and Matilda. Corey, wake up."

Her blonde haired son stirred in his seat as the car came to a stop at the daycare centre. "I'll take him," Joel said to her, releasing his seatbelt.

"No. I'll do this. You know how he hates you doing it." She unbuckled her seatbelt, got out and opened the back door. Her son, bleary eyed, was beginning to look around eagerly for his two friends. "Benny," he murmured.

"That's right petal," she said carrying him through the front doors. "Let's go and find Benny." She put him down and he ran toward the main playing room. A daycare worker was there to greet him. "Let's go find your friends Corey, shall we?" she said brightly, and the little boy grinned at her. Estelle could only look as his tiny, tiny legs disappeared through the door. She turned away. It didn't matter how many times they did this, every time sent a shiver of anxiety through her. She just didn't like being separated for a whole day from her son.

Deep in thought, she returned to the car. Joel had his usual worried frown to greet her. "Ok, he got off ok?"

"Yep," she said, glancing at her watch. "We'll need to hurry now to beat the bridge traffic."

They were mostly silent during the remainder of their journey into the City. Luckily they worked close by each other, and Joel had access to free car parking in his building. Once there, she only needed to walk the two remaining blocks to the Woman's Post head office, the magazine she had started on as a cadet journalist more than a decade ago. Now she was its editor. She pulled out her I-pad and checked her schedule for the day. There was a meeting with the advertising manager scheduled for eight thirty, a mere 25 minutes away. She hoped she was on time. And then was an editorial meeting with the heads of department at ten thirty. Next, lunch with the Editor in Chief, and there was an afternoon brief with legal on the Bannister story they putting on the front cover – a story about a young woman who had been gang raped. It was a brave call to put her on the cover, but it was national rape victim's week and the Bannister woman was topical at the moment, because she had fought back against her attackers and had escaped near certain death. Her bravery was inspiring. It also helped that she was young and beautiful, and someone people could relate to.

"Umm, I've got a busy day honey," she said, without looking at her husband.

"Me too," he said without taking his eyes of the

looming traffic. They would just make it into the city before the worst of the peak hour rush. It wasn't long before he was manoeuvring the Audi into the spot that was reserved for him. He leant over and began kissing her goodbye.

"This weekend, promise me no more bringing home work from the office," he said.

"I won't, if you won't," she answered, playfully.

"Seriously," he said, looking directly into her eyes, "we need some long overdue family time."

She kissed him back then, a lingering kiss. "I know honey. I know. And we will. As soon as the Bannister story is done...but this weekend, I promise no work on Saturday. No I-pad, no mobile, just you, me and Corey."

He smiled warmly and all was forgiven, and she was reminded yet again just how much she was still in love with her childhood sweetheart, even after a decade of marriage. She grabbed her briefcase and headed for the street exit.

"Later," she said winking at him, as he disappeared through the building's car park lift.

He blew a kiss to her as the lift doors closed on him. She quickened her pace, to try and make the seven minute walk in five. Damn, she thought to herself, she should have brought her flats. The new heels crunched the front of her feet, and irritated the bunion that was beginning to form on her right foot. She compensated and put most of her weight onto her left foot. Arriving at her building with exactly two minutes to spare before the meeting with Miranda Bonnington, she flew past her personal assistant.

"Mail, coffee and hold the calls. Thanks Suzie."

Suzie gave her an understanding smile. "Sure Estelle, copy that."

She smiled, shut her door and made herself comfortable behind the huge oak desk that had been at the Post for almost a century. She settled into the leather chair and kicked off her shoes under the desk. Flicking on her computer, she took note of the messages already on her desk and began prioritising them. She grabbed her notebook and pen, a legacy of being a journalist. She took them into every single meeting she attended, whether it was with the Prime Minister or to lunch with the Chair of the Board. Pen in hand, and sifting through her emails, she was ready for Miranda when she walked through the door.

She liked Miranda, but they rarely agreed. Miranda was, after all, the enemy. She was concerned primarily with making her bonus, and ensuring that sales' revenues were met. On the other hand, Estelle was always concerned with preserving the editorial quality of the magazine. They often fought, always over a request for advertorial; the kind of content dressed up to look like a story, but designed to 'sell' the advertiser's products. More and more, the commercial realities intruded for Estelle and she knew that sometimes she had to give into Miranda, but not always.

Today's meeting was over a big pharmaceutical account Miranda had landed, and she wanted editorial support for a four page advertorial feature she planning for them. They were supposed to be talking about what stories might populate the feature and Estelle had made up her mind to be hard arsed about it. It might be an advertorial feature, but it was also going to contain meaningful and helpful content, in keeping with the ethos of Woman's Post. Estelle could have done without the meeting today with Miranda; she didn't really feel like a fight, but she was also conscious of the Board's expectations of her, and that was to deliver a product that brought in revenue. Content was one thing, sales were another and the two were supposed to work seamlessly together to produce the revenue. She sighed heavily, wondering what was wrong with her today. From the moment she'd opened her eyes, she had been dragging her heels. Her PA phoned. Miranda was outside her office. "Send her in Suzie, thanks."

Miranda flung the door open and strode in, on her nine

centimetre heels. Estelle wondered how she walked in them, when she could only manage 'sensible' stilettos with her bunion. She got up and extended her hand.

"Miranda! How are you? Sit down."

Miranda fired back. "Estelle. Long time between meetings."

"Yeah. Sales must be going well," she said, immediately regretting her sarcasm.

Miranda sat down in her impossibly short, straight skirt, and gave her long, honey coloured hair a flick, pretending to ignore Estelle's comment.

"Well, let's get down to business, shall we? You might have heard that I've got the Raine account and we want to do a four page feature. I was wondering if I could have Steph Jones to work on it."

Estelle closed her eyes and forced back the cynical smile that had begun to form. So typical of Miranda to want control, and taking a backdoor approach to get it.

"You and I both know that Steph is one of our lead writers and is actually working on the Bannister story at the moment. What I can give you is Dianna Greenway, but under my direction not yours. You and I also know my journalists do not answer to you Miranda. In any case, you have your sales feature writer, why not use him?"

It was Miranda's turn to smile cynically. "You and I know that he's not up to the job. The Raine account needs a quality writer…"

"Which is why you can have Dianna under my supervision. You'll get your quality."

Miranda sensed she did not have the power in the conversation. "Ok, I can work with that, but I want to suggest the story leads."

Estelle nodded. "Sure, send me your suggestions and I'll consider them."

Miranda was not going to be rolled that easily. "Well I was talking with one of the Board members yesterday and who is also on the Raine Board. Turns out he wants the best possible stories done and I suggested something on their leading market position...written non-commercially of course."

"Alright Miranda, you've made your point. We'll include that story in our mix. But I really need to cut this meeting short – got to get to the editorial meeting later this morning and I've a million and one things to do before then."

Miranda got up, stretching her legs and smoothing her skirt like a panther arising for her morning walk. There was definitely something feline about her, Estelle thought.

"Well, I'll be in touch, via email. Saves time."

Estelle smiled at her. "Yes, that'd be the shot. Email." As she watched Miranda slink her way out of her office, in her nine centimetre heels, she knew she had won the battle but Miranda had also made her point too. She needed to watch that one more closely, she thought. She yawned, and sipped her coffee which was cold. Swinging around in her chair, she took in the view of the city's skyline. What a view, she thought. Immediately Corey came into her mind, and she knew he'd be having little lunch by now.

2 WORK REALITIES

Estelle walked into the editorial meeting, her third coffee for the morning in hand. She had a good bunch of journalists on staff; some she'd worked with for five years or more. There were the usual hard nuts, the older ones generally who'd been trained old school when independence was the lifeblood of good journalism, and when journalists reported for the masses, rather than specific agendas. And then there were the younger Gen Y's. Clever, bright talents but inexperienced. She liked to think that she had the best of both worlds in her team.

"Morning," she said, taking a chair at the magazine's boardroom table. "What've we got?"

They went round the table tossing story leads into the mix for discussion. Estelle liked some, and not others. She was particularly interested in the progress on the Bannister story. "Steph, I want that for the next edition."

"Are we over the legal hoops yet?" Steph asked.

"Umm, almost. One more meeting with our legal counsel and they'll pretty much sign off on it. We need to get Lucy Bannister to identify the third attacker. She knows who it is, but she won't give him up. Somehow Steph you've got to get that."

Steph shifted in her seat. "That's a tough call. It didn't come out at the trial; there must have been a reason for that. The prosecution either didn't have enough evidence, or there's some other reason for it. I'm not sure what it is - only a hunch at this stage."

Estelle nodded. "Let's hear it."

"Well, at the trial there was a testimony that was supposed to be heard, but was withdrawn at the last minute. I'm not sure why. It was from Lucy Bannister's Aunt. We all thought she was making a statement in support of victim's compensation, on the impact of the crime on Lucy, but I'm not so sure now."

"Where are you going with this Steph?"

Steph put her pen down. "You know Estelle, I don't really know. It's just that I think there's something we've missed. I'd like to go back to Lucy for one last interview, but I should be able to wrap up the story by deadline."

"Sure? We can hold it over til next edition? I'd rather break the full story than half of it."

Steph shook her head. "No. It'll be ready, just give me a few more days."

"Ok. You've got it, but keep me posted. I don't want any stuff ups at the last minute."

It was almost lunch time, stories that were allocated were progressing well, and more timely stories assigned. She knew she couldn't be late for her lunch with the Chair of the Board. It wasn't something she wanted to do but it was one of those things you did, with a smile and buckets of charm. Back in her office she ran a brush through her long hair, curling the ends in the hope that it looked at least, semi styled. Applying lipstick and putting on her jacket, she took the lift to the mezzanine level, to the upmarket Italian restaurant in her building. Jim Baxter was at his usual table when she arrived. She wondered briefly why he had called the meeting with her. At best, she met him twice a year, and she had lunch with him last month.

He was the quintessential Chairman of the Board. She guessed he was in his late 60's, silver haired and born into money. His company had only owned the Woman's Post for two years and already it had cut it back to the bone. They were running the business with half the number of staff now. The one department not touched yet was advertising. She didn't much like Jim Baxter's type but the reality was she needed to charm him...for the sake of the Woman's Post. Estelle loved the Post with a passion. It was a passion fuelled by belief; belief in an ideal that the truth should be told.

"Jim, lovely to see you again," she said, purposely not extending her hand. It was too assertive a gesture for the old man. She sat down and was conscious of the feminine way she flicked back her long, dark hair and smiled her brightest smile, lit up with the burgundy lipstick she'd applied a few minutes beforehand. A far off thought almost made her straighten up, stop pretending and be herself, but she didn't.

"So, Jim, as I said lovely to see you again. Did you want to go over circulation figures?"

He smiled to reveal a set of smooth, white cosmetic teeth. It was the smile of a cheetah and she wondered for the first time whether he had called her here to sack her. It was not unusual in today's media climate where senior editors were dispensed with, all with lightning speed.

He leant forward, his face serious. "Actually, no, I don't want to go over circulation figures. The Post is doing well. Circulation is well above our competitor; space in the magazine is still selling at a premium. No I wanted to talk to you about a personal matter."

"A personal matter?" she said, quite puzzled.

"Well, I just wanted to see how you were going. Make sure everything at work...and at home was ok. You're an asset to this company and we look after our assets."

She crossed her legs and leant back in her seat, sipping a wine glass of water. "That's good to hear Jim. Thank you. But I'm still a bit puzzled. I know that your company has an unofficial policy. When we don't hear from you then you are doing everything well, but when we do, well, something is wrong. You know I'm a straight talker Jim, so

I ask you: what's up?"

He took a long sip of his chardonnay. "Well said Estelle, and yes you've always been a straight talker and I admire that. So I'll do the same with you." He paused for a moment. "This is difficult for me because I'm a family man myself. It's come to my attention that you may be juggling being a mother and an editor, and some things might be slipping..."

She was shocked. "Slipping? What do you mean?"

"Now, slow down a bit. I'm not saying the Post isn't doing well. I'm not saying that at all. What I am saying...or asking, is how are you coping with that pressure? It can't be easy. I believe in prevention and it would be remiss of me if I didn't bring this up now."

"Umm," she said, casually looking at the menu "shall we order Jim?"

He smiled again and his teeth almost sparkled at her. "Of course. I can recommend the linguine today," he said.

"Of course Jim."

He motioned to a nearby waiter. "Two linguine's and a salad please, with both."

"So, you asked me if I was finding it difficult to juggle being a mother and a career woman. I'd be lying if I said it wasn't hard, but I'm a professional Jim and I believe you get 200 per cent of my energy, time and motivation."

He took another sip of his wine while the waiter served their linguine. Its aroma distinct and Estelle remembered she hadn't eaten since six thirty this morning. She wound the delicate strands around her fork using her spoon to steady the spiral.

"I'm not saying you don't. Now Estelle you've got the bull by the horns here..."

She swallowed hard and decided against giving the old bastard a piece of her mind. Instead she said: "I can assure you Jim it's not a case of divided loyalties. I'm 100% focused on the Post."

He took a spoonful of linguine. "Good Estelle; good to hear."

She was glad when the lunch came to an end and, as politely as she could, she excused herself when Jim caught the eye of an old colleague. Hurrying to catch the lift, she silently seethed inside. How dare he – old chauvinistic relic, she thought.

By the time she got back to her desk she'd calmed down. Only one more goddamned meeting this afternoon and she was off the hook. The meeting with legal ran smoothly; they just needed to see the updated story and they'd sign off on it. Estelle promised it would be to them by Friday. When 5pm came she was ready to walk the few blocks to Joel's work, and very ready to get into their car and head to Corey's daycare. Now that was the best part of her day, when she saw her son's face for the first time since early morning. She couldn't wait. As she quickened her step to get to Joel's on time, her mobile phone rang. It was Suzie, her receptionist.

"Estelle, Jim Baxter's phoned and wants to speak to you about a circulation matter. What do you want me to tell him?"

She hesitated. "Stall him for 10 minutes and I'll ring him from the car. I can't talk now. I'm in the middle of bloody Pitt Street Suzie."

"Ok, calm down. I'll let him know you are on another call and will call him back."

"Thanks," she said, hanging up. She just about ran to the carpark and was relieved to see Joel waiting for her. "Quick, let's get going. I've got to make an urgent call for work."

Joel looked slightly annoyed.

"Hi honey, how are you? How was your day at work? I've missed you… Can't you try and say something like that."

Estelle rolled her eyes. "Not now Joel, not now, and

certainly not after the day I've had."

And then stopping herself from dragging him into her bad mood, she leant over and kissed him on the cheek.

"I'm sorry honey but the pressures. You know. I've had the Chairman of the Board on my case because he thinks my mothering is interfering with his bottom line; I've had to lock horns with the sales manager who's trying to squeeze me for commercial content and we're doing one of the most explosive covers this month of all time. So, I've had a bitch of a day and it seems like I'm fighting the whole world. The last person I want to fight is you."

He hugged her and kissed her lips softly. "Don't worry. I understand. And no, you don't have to fight me. I'm on your side, you know?"

"I know. I know. It's just that I was wondering where the next battle was going to come from."

He looked at her intently, while turning the ignition. "Honey, you look tired. Are you alright?"

She closed her eyes and put her head back on the seat letting the comfort of being in the car with her husband run through her, mixed with the excitement of seeing Corey and going home soon. She could finally relax.

"I'm ok," she said, rather dreamily. She had to admit she was tired. "Just need a little more sleep. She began to drift off until the face of Jim Baxter ran through her mind."

"Oh damn!" she said sitting forward. "I've got to ring Jim Baxter."

She flicked her mobile open while Joel drove slowly through the city, towards the bridge.

3 SATURDAY AT LAST

Estelle Wainwright heaved a huge sigh of relief. It was Saturday at last. With the week from hell behind her, she decided she would stay in bed that extra 30 minutes. Corey was still asleep in the room next door. Joel was out like a light, and she could feel the heavy tiredness still in her eyes. She needed more sleep.

She let herself drift. The sunshine was coming through her French doors in beams and she could feel it warming the room, even through the doona she liked to still sleep under in summer. Her body began to relax and she hovered in between sleep and wakefulness. The pressures of the week fell away and she moved over so that her body was touching her husband's. It was warm and comforting. Images of Corey and Joel on their trip to the beach last weekend floated into her mind. Happy images of a happy family. She held them, enjoyed them for a minute before the images from her work began their interplay around the edges of the beach scene. The tension returned to her forehead and she began to rub her eyes. Perhaps she would get up after all. She tried to get out of bed without waking her husband.

"Honey…what are you doing?" he said, still with his eyes closed. Why don't you stay…"

She leant over and planted a kiss on his cheek. "I can't. I thought I'd get up and have a quick coffee. Maybe get some washing out before Corey wakes."

He grabbed her hand. "Stay…I'll make it worth your

while…"

Estelle grinned and leapt up before he could catch her again.

"Appreciate the thought but my favourite part of the weekend awaits. Housework." She laughed as she made her way to the bathroom, scooping up her trackpants and T-shirt from the night before. She turned the T-shirt the right way and went to pull it over her head but the action of lifting her left arm was suddenly quite painful. Instinctively, she put her hand to her breast, to a sore painful spot under her nipple. Cyst immediately came to her mind and she mentally bookmarked the thought to have it checked next time she was at the doctor. She had suffered with what the doctor called 'lumpy breasts' since Corey was born and every now and then she developed a cyst which needed aspirating and a biopsy. Every time she marked a long week waiting on the results. Perhaps she should go to the doctor next week, she thought as she began to pick up the clothes for washing they had discarded on the bedroom floor the night before. She had just been so tired when she had been undressing for bed. And Joel had been too. They'd climbed into bed without a second thought.

She grabbed the linen basket from the bathroom across the hall and tiptoed into Corey's room. Her little munchkin was still asleep, his blonde curls surrounding a sleeping, angelic face. His baby fat arms were tucked under his cheeks. She stopped for just a minute to gaze at her child. Her eyes welled up with tears of emotion. She loved her son above all else. Gathering his small pile of dirty clothes and stuffing them into the linen basket, she continued to the laundry. Within a few minutes she had pressed the start button for the wash cycle and she was walking to the kitchen via the lounge room. She stopped to put Corey's red fire truck and coloured blocks into the toy box, and she straightened the magazines on the coffee table.

Estelle had a housekeeper who came in every fortnight to give the house a good clean, but the rest of the time she managed by herself. She took a look round the lounge room, and was reasonably satisfied with what she saw. Not perfect, she decided, but definitely passable. Within moments she was in the kitchen, thankful she had put the dishwasher on last night instead of leaving the dishes until this morning. Her sparkling, gleaming kitchen filled her with pride. Whatever was going on in the other rooms, she always made sure the kitchen was spick and span. It was, after all, the centre of her home, where everyone gathered, where visitors stopped by for a coffee and where she spent her most favourite moments – cooking with Joel, or feeding her growing son. She flicked on the glass kettle and watched while the water heated up to bubbling point. Estelle opened the dishwasher and retrieved her favourite cup and spooned a generous measure of coffee in, leaving plenty of room for milk. She loved her coffee rich and milky.

She sat down at the table and reached for yesterday's paper. Skimming through the news headlines she noticed a piece on Lucy Bannister's trial. The defence had cross-examined Lucy for almost half the day. It would have been the second worst morning in Lucy's life, Estelle thought. That and the morning she was gang raped. She shuddered, almost feeling Lucy's pain. She had almost been raped as a young college student by a boy she thought was her friend, but he went too far and wasn't taking 'no' for an answer. It was Joel showing up unexpectedly at her dorm room that stopped the attack. Joel had been only a friend at that stage, but they had begun dating eventually. He was, literally, her knight in shining armour.

Estelle wondered if her sheer will to get the Lucy Bannister story on the front cover might not be related to the attack in her dorm room. She remembered the shock of the attack, and the helplessness, and then the traumatic memories that followed. Her fear of being alone with a man lasted throughout her second year of college until Joel coaxed her back with his love and gentleness.

She heard Corey stirring and immediately went to get him. "Mummy?" he said, as she walked into his room and scooped him up in her arms.

"Hi monster; how is my little man this morning," she said, using their pet name.

"Rrrahhh," he said, pretending to be a dinosaur. "Mummy…is it Saturday today? Do we have to go in the car to daycare today?"

She smothered his round, baby cheeks with copious kisses. "No we're not monster. Today you, me and daddy get to stay at home."

"All day?" he said, questioning her with his blue eyes. "Can we stay at home all day?"

She looked down at her son, slightly surprised at him wanting to stay at home. Usually, he loved nothing better than to go to the beach, or down to the Manly Promenade for an ice cream or babyccino. "We can stay at home darling if that's what you want."

He nodded, exaggerated movements to make his little point big.

"Ok then. All day. At home it is."

She put him on her hip – he was getting heavy now he had turned two years – and walked past her bedroom. Joel was beginning to stir. "Do you want to have a lie in with daddy and have peanut butter toast in bed?"

He grinned up at her. "Yep please."

Depositing him with a sleepy Joel, she put four slices of bread in the toaster and remembered she hadn't as much as run a brush through her hair since she got up. Grabbing the brush from the bathroom she made her way to the hallway mirror. She looked back at herself. "God, I look tired," she said to her reflection. She noticed the dark circles under her eyes, and dry patches on her face.

'Ugghh.'

Deciding that there was nothing she could do to redeem her good looks without the aid of makeup, she simply brushed her long dark hair, curling it under at the end. 'Pop' went the toast and she hurried to the kitchen. The best part of eating peanut butter toast was to eat it hot. Buttering four slices and cutting two of them into soldiers, she placed the full slices of toast cut in half on a plate for Joel and their soldier versions on a plate for Corey. She grabbed a half from Joel's plate and munched into it as she made her way back to the bedroom.

"Peanut butter toast coming up!" she yelled in time to see her husband being hit over the head with a pillow by her son. "Don't hurt me. Don't hurt me," Joel yelled in mock panic. "The peanut butter monster needs feeding. Mummy, feed the monster." She quickly put a soldier of toast in her son's mouth.

"There you are peanut butter monster. Here's your breakfast; to stop you getting hungry and cranky."

Smiling she sat down on the end of the bed and handed out the breakfast plates. "One for Corey and one for Daddy."

"And one for mummy," Corey said, giving her a soldier of toast off his plate.

Their morning passed amidst a round of washing, housework and gardening. She watched as Joel and Corey dug around the spinach in her vegetable garden and then spread some more compost. They worked so well together; the image of each other and very alike she thought. They were as close as a father and son could be. She said a silent prayer it would always stay like that.

She heard the phone in the background and was tempted to ignore it. The last thing she needed was a call from work; from one of the weekend sub editors with a question they could have easily answered themselves without disturbing her. She let it ring for a second time, and a third and fourth.

"Honey are you getting the phone?" Joel called from the garden.

"Sorry, yeah…"

She grabbed the kitchen line from its station on the wall. "Hello, Wainwrights."

The voice of her best friend Jilly greeted her. "Ok Estelle, what's the problem?"

"Jilly…what…no problems. Where are you ringing from? I thought you were in Turkey, on that aid gig. What are you doing back in Australia and why haven't you called sooner? I was nearly going out of mind with worry when I saw coverage of the riots there…"

Jilly laughed. "It was fine. Really. But yeah, I'm back in Australia for the next few months and I thought if you're not going out today, I might pop round for coffee this arvo. What do you reckon Estie bestie? I've been worried about you…don't know just a feeling."

They had been friends since primary school and Estelle missed her friend. There was no-one on earth except perhaps Joel that she felt so comfortable with. She couldn't wait to see her friend.

"Absolutely," she said "What time? I'll do a choccie cake eh? Treat ourselves."

"Ok then, it's afternoon tea time. See you at three-thirty?"

"You're on," Estelle said blowing a pretend kiss into the phone. "Can't wait Jilly. Seriously, I've missed you."

There was a short silence. "I've missed you too Estelle; can't wait for a chinwag. I've got so much to tell you. See you then."

She hung up and mentally checked off the state of the house. She knew Jilly wouldn't mind what her house looked like, but she was proud and wanted to show her best friend she could cope with life as a juggler with several balls in the air at once. She got out her recipe book and thumbed through it until she found her favourite recipe for triple choc cake. 'Right.' she thought, quick tidy up and get this cake in the oven.

"Joel!" she called out the back sliding door to the garden. "Jilly's home. She's coming round this afternoon." Joel looked up from, wiping away some dirt on Corey's cheek, as he dug with his spade next to his dad.

"Great hon. Know how much you'll enjoy that visit. I might leave you two girls alone for 5 minutes; maybe take Corey to the park. That ok?"

She grinned at him. "Sure…if you want. You don't have to you, you know."

"I know," he said, grinning right back at her with an expression that said, I love you.

She thought in that moment, looking at her husband and son, just how lucky she was.

4 JILLY RETURNS

Jilly came round the back, knocking loudly, excited to see her friend. Estelle just about ran from the laundry where she was folding clothes, ready for the coming week.

"Jilly!" she waved as she approached the glass back door. Jilly was dressed in a purple and red paisley shirt and blue jeans. Her curly hair hung naturally over her shoulders. She was both creative and charismatic; the type that people looked at in the street as they passed not knowing precisely why, but drawn to the stranger anyway. Jilly had charisma, and like all people with that drawing power, she was unaware of her particular magnetism. Estelle unlocked the door and gave her friend a long hug.

"Hey, are you going to let go?" Jilly said.

Estelle stepped back, looking her friend over to see what had changed since the last time they'd met. That was two years ago when she'd farewelled Jilly at the international airport.

"Come on Jilly. You've been away for so long, in a country that's been turned upside down with civil strife. And now you're back, in one piece, at my back door. What do you expect?"

She noticed that Jilly had lost a little weight, and there were the dark circles around her eyes, much like her own, she thought. Ironic, Estelle thought, she didn't consider her life resembled a war zone.

"What is that smell Estelle, like freshly brewed coffee and just out of the oven cake?"

Estelle smiled warmly at her friend, and linked her arm with Jilly's. "Come on. Let's talk."

It was an hour before they even drew breath and they both knew there was so much more to say, but the afternoon was lengthening and Estelle was aware Joel would be home soon with Corey and the evening bath time, feeding and bedtime routine would kick in. She looked at Jilly with real regret their visit was almost over.

"Jilly you're not going away anytime soon again are you? It's just that I've missed having my best friend around."

Jilly reached over the table and put her hand over Estelle's. "I'm not due to go back to Turkey for a few weeks. We can spend as much time together as you've got Estelle. You know that...Look I want to say something, but I'm not sure I should..."

Estelle smiled at her friend and squeezed her hand. "Since when have we kept secrets from each other?"

"Oh, no...I know, not ever really...ok I'll just say it then. Estelle what's wrong with you? You've lost weight and you look like you need sleep and lots of it. I know a two year old is hard work, and working fulltime, but...you just look..."

"Awful," Estelle said, finishing the sentence. "Look Jilly, thanks. I really appreciate it but I don't know. Isn't it normal to be this tired? Yes I'm dragging my feet and I can hardly keep my eyes open after 7.30pm, but isn't this normal with a baby and the kind of job I've got? You've no idea how many arseholes I have to deal with in any one day. That takes energy to keep finding my way around the personalities and the problems. And then there's this constant pull toward my baby when I'm away from him...and the guilt at leaving him in daycare all day."

Jilly patted her hand. "Yes, I know Estelle but I've never seen you look like this before. You're usually so on top of it. Captain of the hockey team, HSC top scorer at school, model student, debating team, all round nice girl. You've always had a lot on your plate, but this is different. It looks like someone has sucked the life out of you. All good with Joel?"

Estelle closed her eyes and drew in her breath. "Everything's alright there Jilly. We're very happy, except for the hours I work, and the weekend phone calls from work...he just wants more of me than I can give at the moment. Corey always comes first, then Joel, then my parents, friends and...well then there's me. No wonder I'm not looking like a model getting ready to step onto the catwalk. I'm flat out accomplishing all the things I have to do in one day, let alone taking a trip to the day spa for myself. So I suppose, yes, I'm looking a bit shattered."

Jilly shook her head emphatically. "No Estie, it's not any of those things I don't think. I mean you look like you need a good, long rest...whether that's away from work or not or maybe ease up on it a bit if you can. It just doesn't look like your normal tiredness. Health? Have you had that checked lately?"

"Actually Jilly I haven't and I've been meaning to. So, end of lecture. I'll go to the doctor next week. There. Can we stop talking about it now?"

Jilly reached over and hugged her. "It's just because I care."

Estelle held onto her friend. "I know."

The door burst open and Joel came in, carrying a very worn out Corey. "Hello you two," he said, as he walked past to the bathroom. "I might just put him in the bath before dinner, or he's going to go out like a light."

Estelle reached for her son. "Honey I'll do that. You've had him all afternoon." She kissed her son's cheek.

"Mummy we had fun at the park. Mummy...daddy's fun too!" Corey said.

She raised her eyebrow in the general direction of her husband and turned back to her son. "Well, daddy will be pleased to hear that."

Jilly pretended to clear her throat. "And what about your Aunt Jilly munchkins. Have you got a kiss for her?" Corey's face lit up as though it was the first time he'd seen Jilly since coming into the room.

"Jilly Bean," he said, rousing from his tired state. "I want Jilly to bath me."

Estelle laughed and handed her son to her best friend. "Looks like Aunt Jilly beats mummy and daddy tonight. Do you mind Jilly? Stay for tea too?"

"Of course. I'd love to, and maybe if Corey eats his vegetables, there might be some room left for chocolate cake." The toddler squealed with delight as Jilly and Estelle took him to the bathroom.

"I'll get his clothes and see where our dinner is up to," Joel said.

"Everything's done hon, on the stove. But if you could mash Corey's vegies, that'd be great."

Within minutes Corey was sitting in a deep bubble bath with Jilly and Estelle coo'ing and admiring the little boy. Estelle watched as her friend played with her baby. If only days could be like this, she thought, surrounded by family and friends, and not the falsities of her everyday work world.

The weekend seemed to whiz by and, before Estelle knew it, she and Joel and Corey were due at Joel's mother's place for a Sunday roast. It was a tradition she remembered from the earliest days of their romance – when they had just begun dating – Joel would bring her to his mum's house for lunch. She would have to endure the sarcasm of Mrs Wainwright, be polite and not raise an eyebrow. A decade on, she was still doing it. As they packed the car with Corey's toys – there were no toys in Mrs Wainwright's upper middle class home in Mosman, only gleaming cedar tables and brass mantles – she wondered when the Sunday roast tradition would end. Her mother-in-law forever found fault with Estelle and with the way she was raising Corey. Estelle suspected it came from Mrs Wainwright's absolute adoration for her son and the resentment she felt toward Estelle for taking him away. But Estelle was tired today. She had so little time to spend with Joel and Corey and she would rather spend the day with them, seeing a movie or going to the beach. She put the last of the toys in the car, strapped Corey into his seat and hurriedly got in the car. They were in danger of being late and Mrs Wainwright didn't tolerate lateness. No, no understanding of a busy working couple's circumstances there, she thought. She wondered how on earth the old lady had raised Joel and his sister, but then she remembered the nanny and the prep school and eventually the private schools.

"Ok honey, I know, we'll be late," she said as she slammed the car door and looked around to check on Corey. She smiled at him, crinkling her eyes. He repeated the gesture. "Right. We're ready. Let's go."

"I'm not going to say anything. I know how much you'd rather be going somewhere else…"

"It's not that Joel, really. I don't want you to feel that you're in the middle. It's just that I'm tired; I've still got a million and one things left to do to get ready for next week, and my weekends are precious with the two men in my life. Three good reasons not to subject myself to the unending torture of your mother's judgements," she said, with just a hint of sarcasm in her tone.

He chose not to take the bait Estelle had laid out for him and, instead, pulled out of the driveway and pointed the Audi in the direction of the leafy north shore suburb; to his childhood home in Mosman. While Corey snoozed in the backseat, the conversation dropped off. They were keen not to wake their overactive son who had needed a nap before lunch. If he slept now, he'd be well behaved for his grandmother and hopefully not damage any of the antiques either with his child's play.

She gazed dreamily out the window, thinking that her life seemed to consist of these moments a lot lately – of her doing something she didn't want to do, or going somewhere she didn't want to go. Estelle really didn't know what was wrong. She was only 32, and at the prime of her career having spent a decade getting there. She had a wonderful family, a husband she loved and the most adorable little boy. Some would think she was at the pinnacle of her career as the editor of one of the most read woman's magazine's in Australia. She appeared to have it all, but as much as outward appearances revealed she was the quintessential, modern day woman who supposedly *could* have it all, she knew in her heart there was something missing. The niggling feeling in the back of mind, well actually her heart, told her the picture was not complete, but she didn't know where to begin to look for the missing pieces. She sighed heavily.

"Want to share?" Joel said.

"Umm, no honey, just thinking of the chores to be done...you know the usual," she said.

He reached for her hand, while keeping an eye on the motorway. "Did I tell you how beautiful you look today?"

"Actually no. Tell me."

"Well I love the way you've done your hair in that bun thing, and those dangly silver earrings – did I give those to you?"

"No, I bought them from the markets last week...but continue..."

"I love the dress. Simple, casual and dressy at the same time. Oh, and I love your shoes, but best of all I love the person sitting beside me."

She smiled at him, still not used to the fact that she had snared such a romantic husband. He had always brought her flowers and, particularly roses, for no special reason other than he could. And he was always leaving little notes for her, with drawings and messages on them. When he wanted to tell her he had managed to put the deposit down on their dream home, he drew a house with a picket fence, and in a heart shaped cloud the message: "yours, mine and ours".

"Thank you," she said, "for just being you."

They were near Joel's mother's house and Estelle closed her eyes briefly, mentally toughening up for the barbs and criticisms she knew were just around the corner. Pulling into the driveway of the two storey mansion, she silently prayed for a bit of help. She had lost her own mother five years ago to breast cancer and she missed her. Missed her desperately. A sharp pang went through her and the tears began to well up. She swallowed hard. She didn't want Joel to see that she would have given anything to be pulling up in her own mother's driveway, and that she never would, not ever again in her lifetime, and there was something so final about that, it brought tears to her eyes. She blinked and composed herself. At that moment Corey stirred.

"Mummy. Where are we?" he asked, trying to rub the sleep out of his eyes.

"We're at granny's darling. Come on, up, up and away," she said, picking him up while Joel gathered the toy basket and the toddler bag.

They walked slowly up to the big, old Oak front door and Joel pressed the deep sounding doorbell. "Here goes," he said, giving her a confident look. The housekeeper answered the door. "Barbara, lovely to see you again," he said kissing her lightly on the cheek.

"How are you?" Estelle said, moving inside and on the lookout for Mrs Wainwright.

"Well thanks, Estelle and how's Corey, he's growing up isn't he?"

"Yes, he is. And where is Joel's mum?" she asked, eager to get out of the hallway and into the lounge room where Corey could begin playing with his toys. He wouldn't stay still for long on her hip.

"Certainly. Estelle, please come in. Joel, your mother is waiting in the drawing room."

Joel moved off and she followed a step or two behind, letting him go into the room first and break the ice. Mrs Wainwright was sitting on the huge gilt edged sofa reading the morning paper. "Darling!" she said, as Joel kissed her on the cheek. "How wonderful to see you. It's just been too long. I can't see why you can't come during the week…like you used to." She looked at Estelle, as if making a point.

"Hello…mother. I'm sure Joel could perhaps come over and see you one Saturday. I don't want to monopolise his entire time, you know," Estelle said.

She offered her cheek for Estelle to kiss. "Estelle, so lovely to see you again." It was a perfunctory gesture, and Estelle had expected it. She bent down to kiss her mother-in-law.

"And Corey? Where's my grandson? Oh, my, he's growing," she said, addressing Joel and not Estelle, as though she wasn't in the room. "Now, come here and give granny a hug," she said, softening her tone and reaching out for him. He slowly stepped forward and she scooped him up. He was the one person, aside from Joel that she showed any affection for.

"Well," she said, "I think it's time for lunch. Barbara…"

The lunch was a drawn out occasion – three courses and then coffee and liqueur. It was far too rich for Estelle. Of course there were the criticisms aimed at Estelle. Corey was being overfed, Joel looked underfed. What was Estelle doing, working fulltime when she had a family to look after? And the daycare. Five days a week was way too much. They stung Estelle, each and every one of them. She was glad when they left.

"I'm sorry Estelle. She was a real bitch today. I'll

MARYANN WESTON

speak to her about her behaviour. It's getting worse. She's got to be pulled up on it," Joel said, later that night in bed.

"It doesn't matter Joel. Really it doesn't. You and I both know that she's never liked me. Never. I remember when I first met her and she asked me where I lived and I said Hurstville. She turned up her nose at that. When I told her I went to Hurstville High, well that was another strike against my name. I really topped it off when I told her I'd been raised by a single mum. I don't think she ever recovered from that."

He put his arm around her and she snuggled into him. "And there you were," she continued, "raised in Mosman and attending Riverview. I mean we were absolute opposites when it came to class."

"My mother's an absolute snob, is what I know."

She laughed. "We both know that. Seriously, I'm not sure I can keep going over there every Sunday Joel. It's not that I can't take her criticism and disapproval of me. I can. But I don't want Corey growing up thinking that's how granny treats mummy, and it's ok. Apart from that it's such a large chunk of my day gone, when I'm flat out and could be at least doing something I like…with my family."

He nodded, squeezing her. "I get it. I really do." He propped himself up on his elbow and looked intently into her eyes. "I'm going to make this up to you Estelle. I'm going to tell my mum that we will be having Sunday lunches at home from here on in, other than the last Sunday in the month, when we'll visit it. But you know what?"

"What?" she said.

"I'm going to let her know that if she doesn't behave herself around my wife, we'll only come on Christmas Eve and her birthday."

Estelle shook her head. "No, that's not necessary."

He nodded his head in answer. "Oh yes it is."

She snuggled into him and before long they were both asleep.

She slept well that night, no tossing or turning, worrying or dreams. Just a straight, deep sleep. When she woke in the morning, she felt the sun on her cheek and anticipated a good day. She knew she was loved by her husband, no matter what and it was a good feeling. She rolled over to get up…to begin the routine of Monday morning and getting back to work, but she stopped suddenly – a pain in her left breast shot through her as she rolled. Her hand went instinctively to her breast to soothe it, and she felt the lump there again, bigger and harder, and less moveable this time.

5 A DETOUR

Estelle crossed her legs in the waiting room of her doctor's surgery. She had chosen to see a female doctor at the same surgery as their family doctor, who was an elderly, experienced man she'd known since childhood. She couldn't explain it, but she had a need to talk with another female; one who knew what it was like to imagine the unimaginable. She glanced around the room – busy mums with snufflely toddlers, elderly couples, and a young teenage girl. All in their own worlds; all with their own lives and their own problems to confront. She picked up National Geographic and began flicking through its glossy pages. She loved the magazine with its lifelike landscape images, beautifully produced and inviting to look upon. A shot of Western Australia caught her eye. The colours were brilliant, red dirt contrasted with blue sky and the corn colours of the Spinifex. She wondered how long it had been since she last went on a holiday and lost herself. Completely.

Her mind drifted back to early adulthood, just after university and before marriage. She had gone backpacking across Australia and had travelled up the coast of NSW, through the northern rivers country and towards the sun. There, the people had an open expansiveness that, along with the sun, warmed you through. She had been a reasonably deep thinker in those days; not that she wasn't now, it was just that the reality of urban living was you rushed from place to place and most of your peers were trying to be somebody. It was almost as if, unconsciously, you just fitted in despite who you might be inside, or what you really might want.

She remembered a particular road just out of Wauchope on the central coast of NSW. She had struggled to get a lift and she was only a few kilometres out of town. It was framed, either side, with gums which formed a canopy over the road. Everywhere, green rolling hills and a fertility that almost dripped from the land, soaked through her senses. Nestled on the right of the road, at the foot of two hills, was a whitewashed cottage, surrounded by trees, its grey slate roof and red door, contrasting with the colours in the landscape. Estelle remembered thinking she wanted to live in that cottage one day. It would satisfy her, that cottage, with her loved ones, this country…for a lifetime. As she looked up at the clock and realised that in an hour she needed to meet with her senior writer in the city on the Bannister story, she wondered just what had brought her to here…to now. Was any of it important – the career, the long absences from her son, the constant pressure she put on her marriage; and the superficiality of it all?

Estelle Wainwright knew breast cancer intimately. She knew her odds too, were higher with a close relative who had died of breast cancer. She didn't dare think ahead to what she would do if she was diagnosed. It had to be a cyst…just a cyst she told herself.

She had held her mum's hand, in a doctor's surgery like this, not so very long ago. Her mum had just been given the results of her biopsy and was told she would need a mastectomy within weeks. Hers was a particularly aggressive form of cancer. Weren't they all, she thought wryly?

Her mother had sobbed. She too knew about cancer, having lost her own mum from it – Estelle's grandmother. Generations of her family's women, dealt a potential death deal, all on the roll of a genetic dice. She had promised her mother they would get through it, that her mum would be ok. She was strong and resilient. She only had to follow the treatment, and they would look into alternative treatments to run parallel with the chemo and radiation. She had looked her mother in the eye and told her they would get through it...but they didn't. The cancer spread and took more and more of her mother's strength and with each passing month, until there was only a shell of resolve left at the end. Death was a welcome friend for her mother, when it came.

Estelle shivered and was suddenly conscious that her name was being called out. She got up hurriedly and walked quickly into Dr Hanier's office. They made polite introductions and Dr Hanier looked at her file. Estelle confessed to the lump which she said would be ok, like the others. It would probably be a cyst.

Dr Hanier sent her for an ultrasound that afternoon and also a needle biopsy. The results would be back in 24 hours. There was nothing more to do than wait.

She managed to get back in time to her office, ignoring the messages that had piled up in her absence. Legal needed the updated story, Steph had been calling – three messages actually in the last 30 minutes – and the Daily Telegraph wanted an interview, on why they were covering the Lucy Bannister case, and 'Accounts' needed the forward editorial budget.

She sat down and swivelled on her chair, drinking in the horizon. It was a warm Sydney morning and the haze of the city had begun to settle on the skyline. The grey smoke of exhaust fumes, the bitumen and the concrete, blended with the air currents of the ocean shore. Sydney was both a cosmopolitan coastal jewel and a repository of pollution, dirt and crime at the same time. Big, sprawling and impossibly diverse, it held the charm of dreams and Estelle had reached hers. The editor's chair behind the big oak desk, in the penthouse suite of offices, atop of one of the renowned inner city building, was everything that symbolised success for her, yet today she felt like time itself was mocking her. The successful dream she'd worked so hard to build was meaningless when it came down to life or death.

"Get me Steph," she rang through to Suzie. "And Suzie, as soon as possible! I want to wrap this up and leave early this afternoon. I've got something important to do." That thing of importance was picking Corey up, getting home early and taking him to the park. She wanted to – needed to - do that today.

Within minutes, Steph was walking through her office door. Steph was an attractive, up and coming journalist. She'd only been with the Woman's Post for three years and she was now their senior journalist. She had a good knack of smelling a story that would sell, for all sorts of reasons. A big picture thinker, she could see the critical points, and bring them together. Her stories succeeded for not just one reason, but 10 and, for that, she was rewarded with promotion after promotion.

Estelle liked Steph. They got on well, easily conversing over a variety of subjects. They had a similar understanding of the news' cycle, knowing it in all its fickleness but prepared to stand above that, and lead the agenda. Together, they were a successful team. Steph respected Estelle's position, a rarity in the newsroom with apprentices always looking for ways to triumph over the master. In the end, Steph may well succeed her as editor, but it was a thought Estelle was comfortable with because Steph had never undermined her…yet. Of course, there was always a first time for everything and she well knew that to have expectations of right and wrong was a dangerous game to play that rarely delivered any winners. Steph had a mass of curly red hair which she usually tied back, but today it hung loosely around her shoulders. The dark rings under her eyes told Estelle this had been a story that had come with huge pressure.

"Ok Steph. Where are we at with the Bannister update?"

Steph brushed her hair impatiently away from her face, a movement that further told Estelle her number one journo was stressed. "I've got it in the bag Estelle. I have, but there's been a complication..."

"For God's sake Steph. Don't come in here on deadline and tell me that." She leant back in her chair conscious of the need for leadership. "A complication? What sort of a complication?"

"Remember I told you that the prosecution subpoenaed a witness then withdrew that? Remember there was some conjecture that there was a third attacker involved that Lucy might have been shielding...for whatever reason?"

"Umm," Estelle said, nodding and intense.

"Well, it turns out that the attacker was Lucy's first cousin."

Estelle drew a deep breath and sat back in her chair. Looking at Steph, as if assessing what was to be done next. She got out her desk diary and fingered through until she reached 'L' for 'Legal'.

"Okay...go on."

"Well apparently the prosecution knew, but Lucy's aunt wouldn't give her son up, so she signed an affidavit her son had been with her that night, giving him a watertight alibi. The whole thing has split the Bannister family in two, and...well...for God's sake! Her cousin, Estelle. Can you believe it? It was his gang; he led the attack..."

Estelle picked up the phone, but kept her finger on the dial tone button. "Have you rewritten the story yet?"

"Yes, with an anonymous source from the prosecutions office on the record about the third attacker."

"Have we named him?" Estelle said.

"No."

"Then let's name him Steph. Let's get the whole lot out. I want Lucy Bannister's testimony though. I want her to point the finger at her cousin, as difficult as that will be Steph, that's the only way we're going with the story now. Can you work that angle, and do it now?"

It was Steph's turn to draw in her breath, hold it for a few seconds and blow it out as though she was expelling a huge tension from her body. She smiled at Estelle, slowly at first, before it turned into a huge grin.

"She's willing to talk Estelle; she wants to see justice done, and she wants to see the neighbourhood gangs stopped but she wants a complete assurance there'll be no legal comebacks on her or her mum. Can we guarantee that?"

"Give Lucy that assurance and get me the story written by close of business today. Leave the legal's to me. This is going to fly…I know it will Steph. Good work."

Steph got up with new resolve. Estelle knew it would be a late afternoon. So much for getting home with Corey early. She sighed and refocused, and dialled the magazine's legal counsel.

6 LATE NIGHTS AND DEADLINES

When Estelle finished with legal, the city's skyline no longer had a hazy afternoon glow, but rather the inner city lights dominated her view now. It was that usual seven o'clock-in-the-evening quiet, when most of the city's office workers had gone home, left their work to take the long public transport ride to the outer suburbs. For those that had driven their car into the city, in increasingly congested roads, the weaving lights on the main arterial roads told Estelle they were all stuck in traffic, for hours on end. This was the price they paid for living in Australia's largest city with its cosmopolitan, melting pot of cultures. It was a wonderful city to live in; the heart of the country perhaps, teeming with new ideas and the best the world had to offer. Food, entertainment…you could get lost in those things while being totally anonymous but tonight it was all merely a reminder that in a home, about 40 minutes drive away, her husband and son waited for her to return. She imagined Joel bathing Corey, struggling with the dinner, and she imagined that Corey would be asking for her. She rang down to Steph.

"Steph, how's it going? Nearly done?"

Steph sounded spent. No wonder Estelle thought. "Yeah, sure boss. Just reading over it, proofing it, making sure there are no holes – trying to protect Lucy. I want to do the right thing by her."

"I understand Steph. You've got 30 minutes. I've got legal standing by. They'll work on it tonight. We'll still make tomorrow's copy editing deadline. Don't sweat it."

"Thanks. It'll be with you soon."

Within 15 minutes she had delivered Lucy Bannister's horror to Estelle's inbox. As she opened it, she began to cringe at the opening few paragraphs. It was a raw and brutal story of a gang rape, but one that had to be told. She thought Steph might earn a Walkley Award for this one, and hopefully it would help Lucy feel justice was done, at least in getting her story out.

Estelle scrolled down, slowly, reading every word. The attack, the indignity and exposure of the court case, having to relive the attack over and over again in a public courtroom, the unknown attacker, the revelation it was her cousin and the shame upon shame for Lucy. The discovery there was an enemy within her own family, one who had caused the attack in the first place. The split in the family, the failure of the legal system and through it all, a young girl of 23 years of age trying to pick up the pieces of a shattered life, forever changed by one random decision to walk home from her local pub one night in the spring.

The story was titled 'Lucy's manifesto'. She typed a 'Confidential' into the subject line and sent it through to the legal team. There was nothing left to do now but go home. She rang for a taxi, and suddenly thought about the tests results that were due in tomorrow. She hadn't even told Joel – best to keep that a secret until she knew what she was up against. She dismissed the thought that would inevitably lead to memories of her mother's last days. "I will deal with it tomorrow," she said out loud to her empty office. She flicked the computer office and opted to wait for the cab downstairs in the lobby. She knew the security guard. He was a likable personality and different from the usual people she mixed with at Woman's Post. His conversation would be refreshing and she looked forward to hearing all about his seven children and his parents back in Serbia, and his old life there. Grabbing her briefcase she shut the door on a long day.

The cab ride home was mercifully quick. As she pulled into the driveway the lights were on in the kitchen, the lounge and in Corey's bedroom. Ah, Joel would be putting munchkin down for the night and if she hurried she could kiss and hold her son before sleep took him from her until the morning.

She went inside as quietly as she could so as not to disturb them, besides she wanted to look into their world, the world she should have been a part of tonight, for a few minutes if she could. She tiptoed into the bathroom and winked at Joel. He had made a huge bubble bath for Corey and he had plastered his head in bubbles and made a beard and moustache for him. He had her hand mirror and was showing Corey what he looked like. Corey was squealing with laughter. She couldn't help herself; she was laughing with them and gave her position away. Corey looked up and squealed with excitement. "Mummy! Look at me. Look at me."

"I can see darling and what a handsome man you are too. You've grown a beard and moustache just like daddy does sometimes."

She winked at Joel again and went and got Corey's pyjamas ready, turning down the vegetables on the stove on her way and also the roast chicken in the oven. When Corey was dressed for bed, she put him in his high chair and the three of them sat down for their Monday dinner.

"How was work?" Joel said.

"Shsh. No work talk tonight. Ok?"

"Fine by me. Absolutely fine by me. Wine?" he said.
"Oh, would I!"

He poured her a glass of Sauvignon Blanc and then one for himself. Sipping her wine, she was contented for the first time in a long day. "Do you know how much I love you?" she said randomly, as though it had just arrived out of the blue.

He nodded. "And you. Do you know how much I love you?" It was her turn to nod.

She turned to Corey. "How lucky are we Joel? No really, seriously, what we have here is so precious, so very precious. I never want to lose it."

He frowned, puzzled by her tone and words. "Hey what's got into you tonight? You're worrying me."

She smiled over her wine glass at him. "Nothing honey. It's nothing." She got up to Corey then, and refilled his milk glass. After dinner, she spent a precious half an hour reading to him, a book about a little boy who handed his clothes down to his soon to be brother, called "He'll Soon Grow Into It".

"Am I going to get a brother?" Corey said through sleepy eyes.

"One day, I hope darling, but not right now. I love Corey and Daddy. Ok."

"Mummy. Sometimes I get lonely at daycare when you and daddy go in the car. If I had a brother, then he could come with me mummy."

She stroked his cheek. "Do you get lonely there Corey?"

"Sometimes mummy."

"But why darling? There are heaps of your friends there," she said.

"But that's not you mummy," he said, closing his eyes.

She leant over and kissed him on the cheek. "Well I'm here now munchkins. Sweet dreams baby."

And with that he was asleep; all thought of a younger brother gone, totally secure in his own little world, she thought.

Back at the table Joel had poured her another glass of wine. She straightened as she walked back to the kitchen, remembering her test results would be in the next day. She debated with herself whether or not to tell him, but he had already dimmed the lights and she kissed him on the cheek instead. "Thank you."

"For what?"

"For just being you. For the dishes, for bathing Corey, for cooking tea, for not ever being cranky when I ring you to tell you I'll be late home, for…a million and one things, but most of all for being my knight in shining armour that day when I was about to be attacked."

He raised his eyebrows. They hadn't talked about that night for years. "Umm. How's the Lucy Bannister story going?" he said, as if reading her mind.

She took a long slug of her wine, as though it would ease the pressure of the last few months. "Ah, well, it's in the hands of the legal eagles now Joel. I've given it my best shot, to try and get Steph's story on Lucy Bannister out there, to give it the most prominent position I can. I've done my best to try and address the injustice, even the scales…It's risky for sure, very risky but it'll either make or break me. Did I tell you that Joel; that if we get sued I'll probably lose my job…"

He cut her off. "Estelle. You're getting ahead of yourself. I'm glad the story is going well and you know what? I don't care if you lose your job."

Her eyes widened. "What? You don't care…what about the mortgage, the car payments, Corey's school scholarship fund, private health, annual holidays…"

"Stop," he said putting a finger to her lips. "All of that…we can sell the bloody Audi. Who needs it anyway? A Ford will do just as well. As for the mortgage, I can handle that. Without the daycare fees and cutting back on the high life a bit. It could work Estelle…if you want to make it work, it could."

She began to clear the table. "I…I don't know Joel. I've worked so hard to get where I am. It's what I've always wanted. I've never imagined myself doing anything else."

He began to load the dishwasher. "Estelle, do you

mean to tell me that working part-time, easing up a bit, or not working at all, and staying at home with Corey wouldn't be what you would want?"

"It's not that Joel. It's just that it's an unknown. Would it be enough? Ok, let's turn the tables, what if I said to you that you could stay at home. What would you think?"

He began rinsing off the pots, stacking them in the dishwasher where they could fit. "Me stay at home, or maybe work part-time?" He looked at her, as if to let her know he was about to tell the absolute truth. "Honestly, I wouldn't mind it Estelle. I love spending time with Corey and I would love to do my Masters. But that's not why I brought it up. I brought it up, to get you to start thinking about options."

"Why?" she asked, looking back at him with just as much of a promise of truth. "Why bring it up now, tonight?"

He stepped closer to her and grabbed her by the arm. "Because look at you Estelle. You're tired all the time; you don't enjoy your work anymore. All you do is rush from here to there and I bet you're just treading water but most of all Estelle, most of all I see how it cuts right through you to leave Corey each day."

They stared at one another without moving. The clock on the kitchen wall ticked over, a contrast against the quietness of the house. "Joel…I don't know, I don't know. You're right; it's all falling apart…" He gathered her in his arms then and she sobbed quietly, the tension of life itself ebbing away with each sob. He kissed her hair and her wet cheeks, trying to make it better; trying to give her a sense of the belonging he felt within himself, knowing that was all that was needed, that his wife had to find where she belonged, within herself. But he didn't tell her that. He knew her very well. He knew she would put it together herself, piece by piece until the whole revealed itself, and then she would know; then she would finally know.

7 LUCY'S MANIFESTO

She heard the phone ring before she heard her alarm go off, which appeared to happen simultaneously as though this would be a day of huge impact for her. She hit the button on the alarm before it woke her husband and son, and then reached over to get the phone. It was her chief legal counsel.

"I've read the story Estelle. We've had a couple of opinions on it. It will be defamatory, but I think we can argue public interest. I think the fact that the alleged attacker's mother was subpoenaed and that is a matter of public record, the testimony from Lucy in court there was a third attacker, and the public prosecutor's source...that and the compelling interview with Lucy. I've sent the letter confirming all this to you this morning by courier."

Estelle was relieved and grateful. It wasn't often the magazine's legal counsel went out on a limb like this. "Thank you David. Thank you."

"Don't thank me. I have to say that what has happened to Lucy Bannister has been tragic, but that girl is strong and she'll be alright. You know I used to be a public defender in the old days. I was glad when this one came across my desk."

Estelle smiled as she hung up. Of all the luck, to get a former public defender. They were the rare finds; the barristers who still acted according to conscience, the advocates and those that tried wherever they could to redress the balance of justice, given that the law was not always fair, nor right.

She quickly phoned Steph to give her the good news, and then phoned production to get the processes started. Lucy Bannister's story was going to make the cover of the Woman's Post, within the week. She glanced at her watch. She would have just enough time to make it to the doctor's for her appointment. She had arranged with Joel to take Corey to daycare. She would take their second car in, the old VW Polo she'd had for years.

Within 30 minutes she was out the door and in the Polo. She drove mechanically to the doctor's clinic in the neighbouring suburb. Estelle hadn't had time to think about the biopsy, but it hit her in the isolation of her car. She wondered what she would do if the test result was bad news. Surely she would know, she reasoned. After all it was her body. No, there was nothing wrong. She would be alright. The red light came into view quickly and she braked, slowing in time to let the pedestrians cross. She really must concentrate, she thought. Crossing the road was a mother and her two young children. She wondered where they were going and what they were doing. Were they going to the park, or to daycare? She thought the former by the way they were dressed – in easy house clothes, and there was no rush about them; no mad, frantic dash. Oh, she had felt guilty on those mornings when she had tugged and Corey's hand, propelling him along to cross the road to the daycare, because she was late for work. Sometimes she had been going so fast, his little legs had struggled to keep up… Estelle felt the tears welling up in her eyes, and she let them come for all the mornings she'd got Corey out of bed in the cold; for all the dinners she'd missed with Joel; and for all the lost hours she'd spent in her office when she should have been at home. Most of all she cried for herself, big full tears that streamed down her face. They were for the rich life she'd failed to live, the one that brought inner knowledge, peace and the sense that her life had meaning, the one that told her she was living the very best life she could live.

For years she had undertaken the long climb up the career ladder, driven by a relentless drive to succeed. Now, she wondered why; what was it that propelled her forward? She searched her inner self for the answer, and she didn't rightly know. Was it some vague idea of feminism, that women were as good as men and it was her duty to prove that? Was it a secret need for power, hidden under the guise of feminism, or was it because as the daughter of a single mother she always had something to prove to herself and the world? In that moment before she stopped in front of the doctor's surgery that morning, Estelle didn't honestly know what the last 10 years had been for. The closest answer she could summon was that she did what she did so that the Lucy Bannister's of this world could be heard. But was Lucy more important than the son she sent to daycare with a cold when he should have been at home in bed, with his mum?

She had no answers today. She dried her eyes and walked, straight backed into the surgery. Whatever the outcome of today, things would change she thought. Life in all its brevity deserved to be lived, for the right reasons.

She hadn't been seated long before the receptionist called her name. Dr Hanier's bright face appeared from behind her door. "Estelle, come on in. How are you today?" Estelle answered mechanically that she was fine and asked the doctor how she was. Ironic, she was exchanging pleasantries with a doctor who held the answer to her mortality.

"The tests Dr Hanier how were they?"

"Sit down Estelle please."

She sat down searching Dr Hanier's face for a sign that everything would be fine but the doctor's face gave nothing away.

"Estelle I'm afraid the results were not clear cut. The

needle biopsy was not definitive. We'll need to do a further biopsy, under general anaesthetic to be sure. We'll do it as soon as you can; this week if you like?"

She nodded, numbed by the news, but strangely calm with it. It was almost as if she was observing herself. She really had expected Dr Hanier to say the needle biopsy was clear, like she had twice before, with the other cysts that presented as sudden lumps in her breast.

"This week…yes…of course. When?"

"I think the day after tomorrow Estelle; depending on whether the theatre can fit you in, but I think it will be fine. There are priorities for this, you know."

"Umm, yes, of course," Estelle answered.

Dr Hanier put her hand on Estelle's shoulder. "Does Joel know you are here?" She knew Estelle's family history, and she knew she was married to Joel.

"No. I didn't want to worry anyone until I knew for sure. I…I wasn't expecting it to be bad news."

"Don't be too premature Estelle. This isn't bad news, merely a need to do further testing because our first test was not definitive." She leant forward, making her point. "Estelle, I would like you to go home now. Take some time off for the next few days. Hand over that magazine to your 2IC, get some rest…and talk to your husband."

She nodded. "I understand…yes, I will. Day after tomorrow. You'll ring…"

"Yes, hospital staff will be in touch to let you know about the schedule, give you the admission details…"

She got up then, and thanked Dr Hanier. She wasn't sure what she was thanking her for. She was suddenly very conscious of the lump in her breast and for the first time thought it might be something more than a cyst. She drove home, mechanically, and was glad to close the door on the world. She turned the shower on, her second that day, and sat down on the tiles, letting the warm water cascade over her until the heat ran out. Towelling herself dry, she put on her pyjamas but not before she took the phone off the hooks and turned off her mobile. She climbed into her bed and pulled the thick doona over herself, closing her eyes. She felt the exhaustion of the past months, perhaps years, seep through her bones. She let the heaviness come, her mind a blank canvas of confusion. Estelle did what she had done as a child; she let the innocence of sleep come, and slipped into a dreamless slumber.

8 THERE'S NO PLACE LIKE HOME

"Estelle, Estelle." She awoke to Joel's urgent calls, before he burst through the bedroom door, worry and concern in his voice and all over his face. "I'm here," she said, through the fog of sleep.

"What are you doing Estelle? Are you alright? I tried to call your mobile. No answer. I tried to call the landline. No answer. What the hell is going on?"

She rolled over, away from him. "It's nothing. Really. I'm just tired. I needed some sleep."

He sat down on the bed and placed a firm hand on her shoulder, rolling her back toward him. "I just don't buy that and you know better than to keep something from me. Now what's going on?"

She sat up then, conscious that she owed him an explanation. She remembered Corey. "Where's Corey. Where is he?" she asked, an edge of panic in her voice.

"It's ok. He's with Aunty Jilly for the evening. I want to sort this out Estelle. This is not like you. As long as I've known you, you've never done this. What's wrong?"

Without looking at him, Estelle began to explain about the tiredness, the lump, and the need for a more detailed biopsy. She watched as the colour drained from his face, and as his blue eyes clouded with shock. At that moment, she felt a deep pang of guilt she hadn't shared it with him.

"A lump. It's a cyst right, you've had them before."

"I don't know Joel. No. It may not be. They don't know. They need to do more tests."

He lay down beside her and put his arms around her. "What do we need to do to get you through this?" His words were soft, full of ownership and they told her she was not alone. He would walk with her, onto whatever battlefield had been chosen. She closed her eyes and sighed with heartfelt relief.

"They want to do a more detailed biopsy the day after tomorrow, under general...a more detailed procedure than the aspiration that was done in Dr Hanier's surgery. We shouldn't worry too much at the moment Joel. It's just that with mum and grandma; this afternoon, I don't know...I just lost it."

He hugged her tightly to him. "Why didn't you tell me before this?"

"Because I thought it was just another cyst, and that it would be ok. I never for one moment thought they would need to do more tests."

He hugged her closely, and whispered into her ear. "Whatever the results Estelle. You know we'll get through this."

She nodded. "I know. I know Joel. Honey, I just want to sleep now, for as long as I can. Will you stay with me until I go to sleep? I don't want to be alone at the moment."

"As long as you need Estelle; I'll be here."

She closed her eyes again and let the exhaustion and shock of the day wash over her, secure in her husband's arms against the aloneness she felt.

Estelle slept then, a dreamless sleep, through to the early light of the morning. She awoke refreshed, and the first thought on her mind was Corey. She dialled Jilly's number.

"Hi Jilly. It's Estelle."

"God honey, we were really worried about you. Are you ok?"

"Yeah, I'm fine Jilly. How's Corey? I'm so sorry you were called in like this."

"Corey's fine Estelle. Please don't worry. Just so long as you're fine."

"I'll come by this morning and pick him up for daycare. I'll explain everything then."

"That's ok Estelle. It's fine. I'm fine, if you're fine."

She hung up and quickened her pace. She felt better this morning, safer and surer that everything would be ok. She kissed her husband and turned the water on in the shower. Stepping into the steady stream, she let the warmth run over her body. It would be ok, she thought, as she looked through the steam and through the window to the green foliage that surrounded their house. She was acutely aware of how much she loved life, that there was so much more to experience, so much to see. It was not her time yet. She would not accept that cancer lived in her body, and that it could take her life, like it took the life of her mother.

She had decided to go into work today, to let the Editor in Chief know about the lump, to tie up the loose ends on the Bannister story and push it through production and finish what she started. She was determined to make sure Lucy Bannister's story was told.

She dressed in black pants and a blue silk shirt, and put her flats on. There would be no formality today, certainly no high heels to pinch her bunion. She flicked the switch on the capp machine and woke Joel with a long, deep kiss that said she loved him for being her rock in the storm, for being her anchor and safe harbour.

"Good morning…dressed for work. Why not stay at home today? Let's both call in sick."

Estelle smiled, her dark hair contrasting with the blue of her shirt. She felt different today. Stronger, more in control. "I don't think so darling. I've got to get the Bannister story to press, but I'll tell you what? I'll take some time off after the biopsy."

He raised his eyebrows. "You never take leave unless it's Christmas."

"That's right. I don't, do I? But guess what? Things are about to change, no matter what the result of the biopsy."

"Umm. What do you mean Estelle...change?"

She sat down on the edge of the bed. "It's quite simple Joel. I'm going to 'declutter' our lives. Remember we used to talk about me working part-time when we first got married, but then the mortgage and the things," she said, waving her hands across the room, "got in the way. The Audi, the expensive furniture; the material things we can do without."

He sat up, intent, listening. "But Estelle your career! What about that? I'm not pressuring you in any way, you know that..."

"I know, but I want to do this for me....and for you, and for Corey, but most of all for me. Now, time to get up or I'll be late for an appointment with my production manager."

They headed over to Jilly's and picked up Corey enroute to the daycare. She kissed her son and told him she loved him. If she could, she would work til 3pm and pick him up early. "I'll see you after your afternoon nap today," she said. His face lit up, telling his daycare teacher that his "mummy was going to spend half the day with him."

"That's right mummy and Corey are going to Manly on the way home for a babycinno."

She held Joel's hand on the way to work. He dropped her at the door of her work. "No walking two blocks for you today," he said, as he leant over and kissed her.

"I'll see you tonight honey," she said.

She spent a busy day working through the production schedule, telling her boss what was going on, that she had a lump in her breast that needed a biopsy and that she would take time off after the procedure, to spend with her family. She no longer felt burdened by the secrets she kept anymore from others and from those closest to her. Somehow the cyst…lump or whatever it was had freed her to think more clearly than ever before. She had stopped pleasing everyone else in her life. It was her time now. Funny, how a crisis can pierce through the confusion that life throws in your way, she thought.

The Bannister cover was powerful, possibly the most significant of her career though that was no longer important to her. What satisfied her was the thought that Lucy Bannister would be one step closer to freedom after that cover was published, free from the hurt that injustice had caused, on top of her rape. And one step closer to bringing the last of her attackers to justice. As she signed off on the cover, she was satisfied with what she had achieved in her life so far but, at the same time, she knew there was more she needed to know, to do and to be.

As she closed the door of her office at precisely 2.30pm, she found her mind wandering to the seaside pier and her son's face when she would surprise him and say he could have chocolate cake with his babycinno. Yes chocolate cake and time with her son; what a good way to spend the afternoon before going home, in the daylight, and beginning the evening's routine.

For a minute she felt like Dorothy in the Wizard of Oz and was tempted to click her heels. In fact, she mouthed silently to herself "there's no place like home; there's no place like home…", as she took the lift downstairs to her waiting cab.

9 A QUESTION SETTLED

Estelle awoke from the anaesthetic in the recovery ward, bright hazy lights becoming clearer until she could focus on them, and the stainless steel environment that surrounded her. The caring face of a nurse loomed into view.

"How are you feeling Mrs Wainwright?"

She nodded her head, and forced a weak smile. "Fine. Thank you."

She touched her left breast, conscious of the faint pain there.

"Just a couple of stitches. Would you like something for pain?"

Estelle shook her head. Within minutes she was being wheeled back to the day surgery ward where Joel was waiting. His worried face greeting her as she gingerly moved from the trolley into a freshly made up bed. She only needed to wait four hours and, if all was well, she could go home. They knew not to expect the results from the breast biopsy for about a week.

When she was settled, Joel gave her a soft kiss on her forehead. "How are you? Much pain?"

She shook her head. "Not much, a little now."

He waived to the nurse. "Can my wife have some pain relief?" Within minutes the nurse had brought over two small white pills. "These will help," she said.

Shortly afterwards, the surgeon came in to check on her. The biopsy had gone well, he said, though she could expect some bruising. He had prescribed painkillers for the next few days to take home, and then told her she was free to leave; to go home and rest. Estelle was aware of his noncommittal tone when he told her he could not predict anything from the biopsy; that was in the hands of pathology.

"Don't have any expectations, but hope for the best," he said.

She wondered what he had meant by that. The waiting would be difficult, very difficult – for her and for Joel. Within the hour they discharged her and were on their way home.

Joel was silent for most of the way.

"It's ok to be scared," she said to him, conscious she had had longer to get used to the idea that she may have breast cancer than he.

He shook his head, and spoke through clenched teeth. "Why Estelle. Why did this have to happen to you? I'm not scared. I'm angry. Angry that out of all the low lives in this world, you had to get this."

She reached for his hand. "You and I both know that we should hope for the best; not think of the worst…otherwise we'll never get through this week."

He nodded, giving her a half smile that said he would try to control his anger. They had decided to spend the evening at home; Jilly had Corey for an overnighter to give them time to be alone. She would pick him up in the morning. Estelle had arranged to take the week off work.
Joel was fussing. He had made a bed up on the lounge for her, so she could be in eyesight and earshot of him as he cooked a simple meal for them – a mushroom risotto. He put the remote in her hand. "Now watch Spicks and Specks," he said, as he went to chop onion and mushroom.

"Ok, ok, I'm zoned out ok? Not thinking about a thing."

However that wasn't entirely true. She kept going over

her life, the busyness, how much she had pushed herself – did any of that cause this to happen? She didn't know. She had tried to stay healthy but the 12 hour days, coping with a young baby, house and husband. Had that been too much stress? After all, the experts all agreed on the effects of stress on the body. Some schools of thought even said cancer could strike after a particularly stressful life event between one to two years following that event. That event for her may have been the heavy grief she felt after the death of her mother. How ironic, she thought, that cancer had claimed her mother and that desperate loss and overwhelming grief might be responsible for taking her life...

She tried to snap out of it and turned on the television. She didn't feel like watching anything much, but there was a rerun of Walt Disney's Snow White. It was just the thing she needed, to be transported into a child's world, to let her imagination flow to a beautiful princess, a forest and seven little dwarves. She looked at the dust on her window sills; she could do with a few dwarves in this house over the next few days.

The days passed slowly for Estelle as she waited for the results of the biopsy. Her life as the editor of the Woman's Post seemed like it had occurred in another time and place. Each morning she dressed in either track pants or jeans, put her hair up and got her little boy ready for the day ahead. Getting up and cooking Corey and Joel breakfast was one of the favourite parts of her day, and then she and Corey fell into their easy routine. They would play in the morning or read books. After an early lunch he would have his afternoon nap. She would, meanwhile, rush about the house cleaning up but it was different to Saturday mornings. This time Estelle had energy to burn. She would swoop into the lounge room, picking up toys, books and odds and ends as she moved toward the kitchen. Once in the kitchen she knew where everything had its place, and she busied herself straightening it up, on her way to laundry to put on the daily load of washing. Within days, the same meticulous way she managed her editorial department, was reflected as she tackled her housework; head on and efficiently. But she enjoyed the routine, the peace and the time with Corey.

"Mummy, are you having fun here at home?" Corey asked one morning.

"Why do you ask that little man? Do you think mummy's having fun?"

He smiled as he put the last of his alphabet blocks on top of the pyramid he was building. "I know mummy. I know you like it at home, better than work?"

She raised her eyebrows, shocked at Corey's maturity. "What do you mean Corey? Of course I love it here at home, with you." And then, after some thought, "Do you like it here more than daycare?"

He nodded with so much meaning, he chin touched his chest and he threw back his head for extra emphasis, on the backward nod. "Yep!" he yelled. "Much better."

"Then I'm glad Corey."

"Me too," he said.

After his daily nap, they would go outside for a walk. Sometimes they drove to the beach and walked up and down on the wet sand, stopping at the shore to make sandcastles, or go paddling. It was a beautiful, full week and she didn't want it to end. It was only in the dark of the night, that Estelle remembered she was playing a waiting game. In the small hours of the morning, when Joel and Corey slept, Estelle would wake, conscious perhaps more so than before, of all she had to lose.

She took the opportunity the early morning hours gave her to think about her life. She no longer wanted to do her job, no longer wanted to be a journalist. She knew she wanted to be home with Corey and be a real partner for Joel, not some absent minded love interest that connected sometimes in the bedroom but rarely over dinner, after an exhausting day at work. Estelle knew her life was changing, that she'd come to a deep realisation; she just didn't know where she was going, nor who she was becoming.

Jilly came over regularly. That helped with the waiting game. Strong, resilient and beautiful Jilly. Estelle often wondered over the week, just what she'd do without Jilly. They laughed together and, at times, cried together. Most of all they were content in each other's friendship and Estelle felt closer to Jilly than any of her remaining family whom she lost contact with anyway. She wished they could go on like this but Monday came round again with a speed that scared Estelle. She was to get her results today, and she needed to let the office know when she was coming back and, theoretically, that would need to be tomorrow. But she just couldn't bring herself to either call the doctor's surgery or her work. By lunchtime, Jilly was urging her to just call work if she did nothing else that day. Estelle knew, though, the call would have to be made to Dr Hanier.

Jilly had come that day and they had taken Corey to the park in the morning. She watched the sun catch his blonde hair, and the way he threw back his head and laughed hysterically every time Jilly pushed him on the swing. She wanted to capture this one small moment and hold it, as though she would never get another like it.

"Jilly I think I should go home now and make that call. Would you mind staying a while here with Corey? I'd rather do it alone if that's ok. Not sure if Corey should be around," Estelle said.

"That's fine by me; really Esty. You go ahead. Corey will be right. Take your time. We'll come home within an hour. I'll take him for an ice-cream on the way home."

Estelle smiled at her friend. Jilly had been there throughout her teenage years, and when she had married Joel. She came back from overseas for Corey's birth, and she'd been there when her mum had passed. Now she was her rock, again.

She kissed Corey goodbye and hurried home. Joel had wanted to be there but she had sent him to work instead. He would finish early and come home, and she was to ring him as soon as she had any news. Her hands were shaking as she put the front door key in the lock. Taking the cordless phone from its socket, she went outside. She wanted to be in their garden, amongst nature, for the news. While she hoped for the best, she knew the worst was not out of the question. She dialled Dr Hanier's number and asked to be put through.

"It's me, Estelle, Dr Hanier. Are the test results back yet?" She gripped the phone hard, and willed it be good news. Her thoughts were always on Corey. What would happen to him, if anything happened to her?

"Umm, Estelle. How are you? Yes, we have your results…"

"Please just tell me Dr Hanier. It's been hell waiting this week for them."

"Sure. I understand Estelle. The results are back and they are clear. It's a cyst. You're going to be fine."

She couldn't hold back the sobs then. "Thank…you…you've no idea…what a relief it is…"

"I don't Estelle, but I can imagine. We would however like to keep an eye on things though, for a few months, just to be sure. You've had a lot of cysts over the last few years, and with your family history…well it's just wise we do that."

"Yes…I understand. I'll book the necessary appointments…thank you again Dr Hanier."

Estelle hung up the phone and walked to the kitchen sink, and began to wash up. She didn't know why she was doing that when they had a dishwasher, only that she should keep busy. She washed up every single dirty dish in the house and then began on the glass ornaments. Next she moved to dusting and had every window sill spotless by the time Jilly came back. Jilly came in the back door and their eyes met, Jilly searching Estelle's face for signs of the worse.

"It's ok Jilly. It's all clear."

"Thank God," she said, letting Corey through. Estelle's son flew to her legs.

"Mummy!"

Estelle thought it was the sweetest sound. "Joel, I must ring Joel."

She dialled his number. "Honey?" he said, picking up the phone quickly.

"Yes, it's ok Joel. There's no cancer."

"Thank God Estelle. Thank God." There was silence then, and Estelle had to break it. "Darling, are you ok?"

"...Yes. I'm fine...just relieved. God. Thank God. I'll be home soon honey. Thirty minutes, and I'll bring your favourite wine. I want tonight to be special after the hell of the past few weeks."

"Ok Joel. I'll do something nice for dinner...we'll celebrate." She blew him a kiss down the phone and hung up.

"Well, that's that," Jilly said.

Estelle put the kettle on, and sat Corey in his high chair with a tub of yoghurt. "Cup of tea?"

"God yes!" Jilly said, with such enthusiasm that Estelle got down the teapot. No teabags today; the real thing would do.

"Well. What now my friend...now you have the world at your feet again?" Jilly said.

She smiled, a half smile that was had traces of relief and weariness at the same time. It wasn't lost on her friend.

"What's wrong Estelle? I thought you'd be over the moon."

She handed her friend a cup of tea. "Oh, it's nothing Jilly. I am over the moon, but I've done a lot of thinking this week about what I would do when I got the news – either way."

Jilly sipped on her tea. "What do you mean?"

"Well I mean, what I would do with my life. I'm not entirely satisfied with it Jilly."

Jilly looked at her friend over the rim of her teacup, surprised at Estelle's admission. "I wouldn't have thought you weren't satisfied Estelle. You have a gorgeous son, a wonderful husband and home…what else is there?"

"That's precisely it Jilly. I have all those things and I'm never home to enjoy them. I mean what's the point of it all, the career, the achievements, the status, if I can't enjoy my son's childhood, or be here when my partner comes home to enjoy our time together. And Jilly life is so short. Surely you can understand…"

Jilly held her friend's hand. "There's no need to explain Estelle. I understand. You might wonder why I travel the world; go into strange countries and places, as a volunteer. But it's simple; it's where I belong. Where I feel it's my place to be and, when I'm in Australia, I think about the aid centres, and the children without education, health and even something as basic as clean drinking water. It's only when I'm there, on the spot and helping these kids that I feel at home. So I make it easy on myself, I go where my heart wants me to go and whether that makes sense or not in my head doesn't really matter because it's the heart you have to satisfy."

Estelle leant over and hugged her friend. She had understood her so well, but then Jilly always had.

"Now Estelle, I'm going home because I know Joel will be home soon…and you've a lot to talk about."

She nodded. "I'll see myself out."

It wasn't long before Joel's Audi pulled up in the garage. Estelle had put Corey down for his afternoon nap. Her husband came through the front door as though the wind itself was carrying him. "Estelle, Estelle."

She ran to meet him. "I'm here. Joel." She hugged him as tightly as he was hugging her.

"I don't know what I would have done if it had of been cancer. I don't want to think about it," he said.

"Well it's alright now. We don't have to think about it. Come on, I've still got some tea left in the pot. Would you like a cup?"

He produced a bottle of wine from behind his back. "Actually, I thought we might share this."

She smiled. "Why not? I've got a lot to talk to you about."

He looked puzzled.

"Oh come on, it's ok, just that I want to talk to you about the future...our future."

She sat him down, and poured two glasses of wine, handing one to him and taking a long sip out of the other. "These last few weeks have given me the time and motivation to think about our future Joel...I suppose the cancer scare, the pressure of work over the past year; and Corey's growing so quickly..."

The smile Joel had worn when he entered the house earlier that day had gone. "What are you trying to tell me Estelle? I thought we were going to celebrate..."

"Honey don't interrupt...just let me finish." He folded his arms. "As I was saying, I have been doing a lot of thinking about our lives, and about what's best for us...for me in the future. I want to give up work Joel...well at least fulltime work."

He nodded. "Why Estelle. You've worked so hard. Don't do it for us. We're fine. I don't want you to give up on your dreams."

She shook her head. "I'm not doing it for you Joel, and I know Corey is ok...I'm doing this for me because it's no longer enough to chase a career. It all seems so silly in comparison to my health, my life, my child's wellbeing. I haven't felt myself for a long time Joel, and the cyst, the cancer scare, well it's made me realise my life has more meaning than the endless treadmill of trying to succeed at work. It just doesn't have any point for me anymore."

He came over and sat beside her. "What do you want Estelle. Do you know?"

She nodded. "Yes, I think so. I want some time to find myself. For as long as I can remember I've always been trying to get somewhere or be something, and I don't really know who I am Joel. After all these years, I don't know who I am. I just know that I don't belong anymore in the business world. Oh, I'm not saying I stop doing everything. I'd like to write a few articles a week for the Women's Post, but I don't want to be constantly in that environment. I want to be able to hear myself breathe, to watch the sunset, and not from the inside of a car, stuck in traffic and panicking because daycare is about to shut for the day. I want more Joel and if I have to do with less money to get that, then I will. But I need your support."

He looked her in the eyes and he never wavered for a single second.

"I want your happiness Estelle, and I'm here by your side for as long as you'll have me. You ask where you belong. You belong here with me and Corey."

The sun was setting behind the suburban skyline. She took Joel's hand in hers and led him out the door to the garden. They sat on the love swing she had bought last Christmas and rested her head on his shoulder.

"We've come a long way Joel, haven't we?"

He nodded. "It's you who has come a long way Estelle. You and you alone."

She looked up at him. "I think that is because I'm starting to feel I belong Joel. I belong here and now, with you and Corey."

The sun dipped below the horizon and dusk fell on the Wainwright home, a belonging place for that night and many years to come.

BOOK 3

JILL'S STORY

1 A POSY OF LILACS

She placed the delicate posy of lilacs on his coffin before it was lowered into the ground. He had loved to garden and the heady scent of the October bloom had always brought memories of his childhood. She wanted to fill his dark grave with the scents he loved best. She couldn't bear to watch the disappearing coffin, so she turned away, a lump in her throat, hopeful no family members would approach her when she could barely speak. She wanted a moment alone to control her grief, so she could look up and talk to them all, tell them she would be ok. She turned away to face the hillside and listened to the priest reciting the graveside prayers. Oh yes, he would be accepted into the Lord's house on angel's wings. He was, after all, a good man.

They had been married 40 years, though he was older than her by 10 years. Enough time for death to take him first and leave her widowed and alone. She remembered their first date, still. It had been a picnic at his uncle's farm. It was spring she recalled, and what a spring it was, coming as it did after three rainy seasons. The ground was jumping with life and she could feel the fertility of the ground beneath their picnic blanket. She even remembered their first real meal together – crusty Italian bread and thick wedges of cheese, fresh ham and billy tea. They had been so innocent then. She was shy by nature and those early adult years had not been easy for her. One on one she showed her true self, but within crowds she would clam up, anticipating the end of her ordeal when the evening was at a close, and she could return to the safety of her home. But on that first picnic, she felt strangely at home with him; this man she hardly knew.

Bill Bridges was a man's man, but he made an exception around her. She knew this; knew that he was putty in her hands, but she never used it against him, never. She wasn't sure when she fell in love with him, whether it was on that first springtime picnic as they munched on the most wonderfully tasting bread and cheese, sipping the tea so that the flavours mixed together, so typically Australian, or whether the love came later. It had been so long ago. The tears ached at the back of her eyes as she recalled that picnic, surrounded by the wild daisies and the gentle hum of springtime. And now, as the coffin disappeared into the ground, the dull whirring of the mechanical gears was the only sound aside from the quiet sobbing of his two children; their two children. She struggled to remember…all their special times together.

They married quickly, within six months of that first spring picnic, and were so in love by then. Jill and Bill Bridges. It always had a nice ring to it, like they were meant to be together. And perhaps they were. She had had a good marriage, plenty of passion in the beginning and they had shared the good and the bad, like any strong couple. What affected her certainly affected him and vice versa. That was the way it was in their marriage, a symbiotic partnership. When she was struggling after the birth of her first child – postnatal depression they said – life was equally bleak for him. When he was wronged by a business partner, that man who long after remained nameless in their household, was her enemy too. In sickness and in health, was never truer for them. They even suffered the same ailments. Two peas in a pod, her mother had said, and she was grateful she had found love in this lifetime, from the beginning.

Their two children had come quickly, one after another, a boy and a girl, their pigeon pair. Life had been complete. That wasn't to say they didn't work hard. They did, for every penny they earned, and saved. They had made their home in a modest; three bedroom brick veneer in a small country town a couple of hours from Sydney. It was a town where everyone was known to everyone, and they had become fixtures, joining in the various clubs and, in her case, the women's groups. She knew she was particularly rated for her cooking. It didn't matter what she cooked, she had that special touch. Her pumpkin scones were well known at the various fundraisers over the years. Jill Bridges' pumpkin scones, she thought ruefully. Was that the contribution she would be remembered by? She wondered how Bill would be remembered.

He had set up his own mechanic's business not long after they had married. They had debated the risks: was it better to work for someone else and play it safe, or take that leap of faith on their own. She supposed being married had given Bill that extra courage because he handed in his notice to the largest mechanic business in their town, where he had worked since leaving high school some 10 years before and rented a small, rundown shed on the edge of town. It had been hard at first, and she had worked extra hours cleaning at the local motel just so they could get by, but little by little their business grew, and now it was the biggest in town, run by her son Jeff.

Memories. She turned back to the graveside to see the coffin firmly planted in the ground. She was not expected to watch the earth being thrown over it. It was time to go. Her son and daughter Ellen were approaching but she had no desire to leave Bill. The tears came and she let them fall down her face, making no effort to dab them away with her handkerchief.

"Mum?" Elle said, in a particularly soft tone for her.

She glanced at her daughter, noticing the grief that weighed her down. Unlike Jeff, she was close to her father.

"I'm ok Elle. Just give me a minute." Her voice was stiff and formal. She was not as close to her daughter as she was to her son. Funny how that went, she thought, that Elle was the apple of Bill's eye, while Jeff understood her, and was distant with his father. Family dynamics were at best, fathomable but not fully understood.

She reached out for her daughter's hand, bonded as they were in that moment by their grief. Jeff approached with his wife Narelle, a pretty young girl and smart too. It was a good partnership.

"Mum, it's time to go," Jeff said, placing a firm and supportive hand on her arm. "Everyone else is leaving and we should be down at the club to greet them."

She looked at her son, wondering about his grief. He didn't have the easiest of relationships with his father. They were too similar, both men's men and as stubborn as each other. Jeff had taken over the business five years ago, when Bill's hands and knees were crippled with arthritis and the dusk of old age had begun to fall. It hadn't been an easy transition for her husband. He had built the business from the ground up with the sweat of his youthful years etched into every brick and mortar, every contract they had ever won, and into the all the relationships built over 40 years with workers, clients and the townspeople who supported them. He had resented Jeff's new ideas at first, distrusted them and rallied against them. They were, after all, not his and he loved his business almost as much as life.

But never as much as her, she thought. She had been his one true love, and he would have sacrificed it all for her had she told him to. She turned back to Jeff, forgetting the children were waiting on her.

"You two go and be there to greet our guests. I need a moment alone…to say goodbye. I'll be alright, just leave me be…for a minute."

They were puzzled and worried by her request, reluctant to leave her but Narelle stepped forward. "Leave her Jeff...Elle. She needs this time. We can arrange with Father Percy to drive her to the club."

So they left her alone with her husband. The grave diggers were starting to shovel the earth over the coffin. She watched as the clods of dirt fell softly onto the red ornate cedar of the coffin. She pictured him in there, sleeping peacefully. He had died without any pain, knowing it was his time, but reluctant to leave her. He had held on, long after the doctors thought he could, and they had tried to make the best of those last few months. She had fitted their home out with rails, and non slip matts in the bathroom, and a special bed. They had oxygen cylinders in the bedroom and the lounge room, and Bill had used a walker until he no longer had the strength to. Then they had used a wheelchair. She wanted to keep him in his home, as long as she could manage and, with palliative care, they had done better than predicted. Bill had only been taken to hospital to lie in his deathbed two weeks before he passed.

"Thud, thud, thud..." She should go now before they finished, and there was only a mound of newly turned earth to mark his grave...until the headstone came. She reached into her bag and took out an old black and white photo of the two of them taken on the day of their first picnic. The faces of two young lovers stared back at her, hardly recognisable now...except for the eyes. Real joy and a growing love were there in the depth of their expressions; windows to the future. Momentarily she paused, drinking in the familiarity of his face and the mischievous humour always at the edge of his expression. She put her lips gently on his photographed face and kissed him softly. Kneeling down, she placed the photograph in the dirt as a talisman for him, so that he would know he did not need to make his journey alone. "I'll always be with you Bill," she whispered softly.

The grave diggers had paused out of respect to allow her to say her last goodbyes. She got slowly to her feet and nodded stiffly to them, wanting to maintain her dignity. She knew that now people would be watching her, alone, ageing and vulnerable. She knew that without Bill at her side she would need to struggle to keep her freedom. She felt the pain in her hip. It had been replaced three years ago and she feared the other hip would need replacing. She walked slowly to the priest's car. Father Percy was waiting patiently for her.

"I know this is hard for you Jill," he said, gently, "but Bill was a good man, and he is resting with the Lord now." She nodded, afraid to say anything at all in case she began to cry again, and could not stop. The Lord gave her no comfort today, none at all. Rather, she felt only anger that she had lost her love, and at the prospect of the lonely years to come. She took a deep breath and got into the car, letting Father Percy take over the job of getting her to the wake where her children would be waiting with the many of the townsfolk who had come also to say goodbye to her husband.

She wondered how she would get through the afternoon, and dug deep for a resolve. But what else was there for her to do. She would go home tonight to their empty marital home, perhaps switch on the TV to blot out her thoughts. She would not be hungry and would put the kettle on for a cup of tea, one cup not two, and then when she felt the heaviness and mercy of sleep come, she would go to their bed and lie there in the dark, conscious of the empty space beside her. And that would be how it would be in the long coming months, empty spaces where he should have been, and always her, feeling only half complete as though a part of her was missing. And it was.

2 A SMALL BIRD'S SONG

It was dawn and she awoke to the sound of the same small bird outside her bedroom window. No matter which room in the house she sat in, there was the bird with its haunting whistle. She seemed to remember it began whistling at around the time Bill got sick. She was now taking more and more notice of it and had begun talking to it. She watched the ease with which it flew away and she wished at this moment that she was like that bird.

She had seen many lonely dawns since Bill's passing. Some of them transported her to other times and places, others were a reminder of the long day ahead, and one or two had made her wish for newness. Life had been the same for months now and she had forgotten what it was like to face new circumstances, and be excited by that. She looked about her bedroom and saw the same scene she'd woken to for 40 years. The house was unbearably empty. They had put on extensions over the years and what was a three bedroom home had become a five, with no end to the living rooms. It was much too big for her simple needs and she knew she had to sell it. The real estate agent was coming this morning.

She swung her legs out of bed. She needed to get moving. Immediately her foot hit the ground she regretted her decision to get up. Pain shot through her foot, all the way to her left hip. The arthritis had been getting worse and she really needed to think seriously about moving to a warmer climate; but that would mean leaving Jeff and

Narelle, her favourite granddaughter and her new grandson. Elle was settled into her career in Sydney as an investment banker so she didn't see much of her...whether her career focus was responsible for that, or just her general estrangement from her mother, was another thing. She didn't know why but they had never got on – like water and oil almost, repelling each other's ideas, opinions, values...and, as a result, they had learnt that to keep the relationship viable, spending time together should be limited. Lately though Elle had been suggesting Jill visit the local nursing home to take a look at the units there. One bedroom, a small lounge room and kitchenette and a balcony that led on to a patio garden. It wasn't so bad, Jill thought, but she knew that it was too soon for that. She liked to think that she still had living to do and she wanted to do that, drink in the newness of the experiences and take them into her soul. She believed that every human being learnt something until the day they died. She had seen too many people of her age close down in arrogance, stubbornness and perhaps fear, and become shells of their former selves. That was not going to be her.

She moved off to the bathroom and took a long, warm shower, running the soap over her old body, noticing the sagging skin and the wrinkles, and occasionally finding some part of her body that retained a vestige of youth. She sighed, remembering all the challenges she had been through in her life and thinking old age was perhaps her biggest challenge. She towelled herself dry, careful not to chaff her papery skin – so many considerations to be made now, such physical frailty, she thought.

The real estate agent was due at nine o'clock, so she had enough time to boil an egg, make a pot of tea and go for a short stroll. She liked to walk down to the park each morning, sit for a while and watch the families commuting to work. It gave her a sense of belonging to society still, even if it was on the perimeters.

Jill was back in time to greet the real estate agent, a young woman in her 20s who had no idea that one day she would age, just like Jill. So much disrespect for the elderly, she thought, but perhaps that was because young people needed to be as far removed from their fate as possible, and it helped to reduce old people to nothing in order to forget. Nevertheless, she was polite to the woman.

"Well, what do you think of my home Ms Donaldson," Jill said, after a short tour of the Bridges' home.

"Please, call me Cameron. We'll be having a lot to do with each other over the coming months and Ms Donaldson is way too formal. The home, yes it has potential with a bit of remodelling to modernise it. It's large and will suit the tree changers wanting a decent sized family home..."

Jill sat down at the table, suddenly overcome by fatigue and a faint feeling of nausea. "But I didn't say I definitely wanted to sell yet...Cameron. Your visit is only a preliminary step and selling is by no means a foregone conclusion."

Cameron tapped the side of the table with her finger, a sign of impatience Jill thought and then sat down opposite her.

"Jeff has already explained to me what it's been like for you here on your own since your husband died...I mean passed on. He says it's not healthy, or even safe for you to be on your own."

Jill noticed the whistling bird had come back and landed in the tree near the lounge room window. It began its usual routine.

"Oh, what's that sound? A little bird singing!" Cameron continued. "Did you realise that Golden Dreams Retirement Village has a lovely terraced garden, patio area outside all of the units. Of course you have to share it with other residents in the village, but why would anyone want to be on their own at your age and stage..."

Jill automatically stood up, as if to project an aura of

power she didn't feel. It was so hard to get her point across these days.

"Ms Donaldson...I mean Cameron. I haven't said anything about moving yet, in fact I haven't decided to sell..."

"But your son said..."

"Never mind what my son said," Jill interrupted. She was losing patience with the pushy agent now. "Thank you for coming out to value the house but my house will not be going onto the market until you hear from me. As far as I know I'm still in charge of my own affairs, and this is still my house."

She could feel the blood rushing to her face and her heart pounding. Ms Donaldson stood up and moved towards the front door. Jill followed as if propelling her out the door from behind. She turned back before she stepped outside the door.

"I've obviously offended you Mrs Bridges. I didn't mean to do that. It's just that I was told it was a foregone conclusion that you were going into the retirement home." Jill smiled and gave Ms Donaldson her best direct stare. She had been known for her piercing looks when she was younger and she summoned one of those from her distant past.

"There are few things in this life Ms Donaldson that are foregone conclusions, as you say, and I'm in charge of my affairs still, so no I have not made any decisions about my future at all."

Cameron Donaldson gave her long blonde hair a stylish flick and looked at Jill strangely, as though she had met a ghost. She thought the old lady had more nous than she showed outwardly. "I understand. I will not bother you again and will tell your son he needs to discuss this with you. Have a good day Mrs Bridges."

Jill closed the door on the real estate agent, secretly looking out the window so she could watch her walk down her garden path in her glimmering gold, high heeled shoes. "Ouch," she thought. "How does she walk in those without breaking an ankle?"

She glanced at the old hallway clock and noticed the cobwebs around its edges. It was nearly 11am and she needed to get ready for the barbecue at her son's place today. She rehearsed their conversation mentally, pulling out her faded denim jeans which she still occasionally wore, and a purple shirt. Now that would shock them but who decreed old ladies had to wear floral dresses anyway? Bill used to love it when she wore her jeans, as they both were teenagers in the 70's, an era where freedom was not just the ideal but demanded and lived by. She pulled her hair out of the bun she had styled earlier this morning and let the white hair flow freely over her shoulders. Umm, she would give them all something to think about. Turn the tables slightly so they would have to acknowledge she was still capable of making decisions.

She stepped into the jeans, having to admit that the roughness of the denim was not the softest of materials she had worn in the past few years but, twirling around in front of the mirror, she had to admit the look was perfect. So much of the way she was treated by people came down to external appearances. If she looked like an old woman, she was treated like one. If she looked like her own person – in jeans and purple shirts – then people tended to respect her more. Superficiality, she thought with disgust. But she was in a position now where she needed to get smart, not stubborn and cynical – that would get her nowhere. No she needed to be smart to be free.

Jill Bridges drove her car to her son's home. It was a sprawling, multi bedroom and bathroom mansion on the edge of town, built on a block of land Jill and Bill had purchased with the same idea in mind: to build a mansion to look over the town so the people within would have no doubt about the Bridges' elevated social position. But they had never gotten round to it and remodelled their original home instead. Neither she nor Bill wanted to leave the family home behind for the bricked expanse of a house that held no memories for them. And when it boiled down to it, they weren't all that interested in status after all.

She was careful going through the front gate in her car. A few weeks ago she had driven too close to post and sideswiped her side mirror. Jeff had looked worriedly at her when he saw it hanging off the side of her car but today she negotiated the narrow space between the two posts successful and pulled up unscathed at her son and daughter-in-law's home. Immediately her grand-daughter ran out to greet her. How she loved Sara Jane. She was all of seven years old and as bright as a button. Jill always got the impression Sara Jane could understand what she was thinking. She had been their first grandchild, and she and Bill had absolutely doted on her. As a result, Sara Jane had been very protective of her grandparents and more so of Jill now she was on her own.

"Nana!" she yelled as she ran toward the car. "Nana, are you staying all day?" she demanded.

Opening the car door, Jill hugged her tightly. Sara Jane reminded her so much of herself. She could see that in her green eyes, but she could also see Bill's firm chin and the decisiveness that accompanied it. Sara Jane was extremely artistic, something she had inherited from Jill's mother, and with it came a sensitivity that immediately honed in on Jill's mood.

"Nana why are you dressed like that?"

Jill placed both hands on Sara Jane's shoulders and looked directly into those green eyes, which were wide with questions. "Well Sara Jane, these are the clothes I used to wear when I was younger. It's not that I want to feel younger; it's just that somehow I feel stronger in these clothes. Do you understand?"

Sara Jane smiled her little mischievous smile. "I know

Nana. You want mummy and daddy, and everybody else, to see you...to really see you."

Jill hugged her granddaughter to her. "That's exactly right darling. I want them to really see me."

Holding Sara Jane's little hand in hers, they walked round the back to the barbecue area and the guests that were milling round. She spotted Jeff deep in conversation with another of the town's businesspeople. He was part of the younger generation of movers and shakers in the town. She and Bill were yesterday's heroes, fondly remembered but irrelevant nevertheless. She walked towards Jeff hoping to talk to him at some point in the day about her plans for the future, though why she needed to consult him she didn't know. Then she saw him look towards her, concern in his face, worry creasing his brow. He was, after all, her son. She would be gentle with him today, she thought.

3 TO THE SEA

Jill glanced out the window at the north coast scenery. It was green; greener than she remembered. It had been a lifetime ago since she last took this trip. In her 67 years she had visited her older sister periodically. While they got on, they were far too similar to be too close. Maeve was also from the old school, of doilies and rose patterned teacups and lace overlays over lounge room chairs. Jill, on the other hand, was not one for stuffiness. Her home was modernised several times over during her marriage, and she liked bright colours and open, airy spaces. She didn't like to be boxed in by conventions which were only someone else's rules when it came down to it.

But she felt the need for family now. It had been six months since Bill's passing and the grief was still raw, tangible and dark. Her nights were filled with sleeplessness and incoherent dreams of fragments of their life together. Forty years of marriage were being replayed in her subconscious, bits and pieces, and nothing making sense. It was as if her emotions were jumbled, and the jumble anchored by grief. She wondered when it would pass, and when living with herself would begin to get easier. She had spoken to Jeff at the barbecue the week before last and he'd agreed that she should go away – have a complete break – to think about her future. When she'd questioned him about what he meant, he merely shrugged and said she could not go on living in that 'big old house'. That it wasn't healthy for her to be alone. She had looked at him in astonishment, dreading what might come next. She had no desire to live with him but he had surprised her when he mentioned Golden Dreams Retirement Village. He'd even made some phone calls.

She had stiffened then and with a straight back and firm voice told him that she would determine where she would live, not him. He had given her a wounded look, to let her know she had hurt him with her rejection. They had come to a compromise. Jill would visit her sister on the north coast and take some time to think, away from the home she and Bill had lived in for 40 years.

The train guard announced they'd soon be coming into Port Macquarie. She would get off there and take the bus to nearby Wauchope, a quiet, seaside rural community where Maeve had lived for most of her adult life. She noticed the countryside had become almost rainforest like and she marvelled that such fertility could be so close to sand and beach. She had always liked the climate of the north coast and found its warmth soothed her arthritis in ways the cold of the NSW southern tablelands did not. Winters were harsh in her hometown and she was paying the price in old age for her decision to make her home there. She felt the train slowing and she got up, stiff after the long trip. A young man in the seat across the aisle did not let her struggle to get her bag down, instead reaching up for it and placing the wheeled suitcase at her feet with a smile. She returned it warmly, grateful for his kindness and good manners that asked for nothing in return.

Within minutes she was pushing her bag to the bus stop at the train station and, consulting her timetable, knew the bus to Wauchope would be along soon. She sat down in the bus shelter and took out her book, an interesting story of a woman who cooked exotic dishes for her friends based on their emotional needs. Her dinner parties were designed to enlighten and restore – a novel idea, she thought, but it appealed to the love of cooking in her and she was enjoying the narrative, a special blend of ingredients for love lost another concoction to restore self esteem and, her favourite, a nine course banquet to ease grief. She smiled as she opened her book; if only a banquet would ease the empty space in her heart where Bill should have been…

Her bus pulled up and she got on. She was anxious to get to her sister's place after the long trip from home which had begun at four o'clock that morning. While she wasn't quite sure why, she had the feeling her visit would be important.

Within 10 minutes she was in Wauchope and she decided to walk the five minutes to her sister's house. Wauchope had changed since she had last visited. It had grown, become modern with its proximity to the seaside, but it had lost none of its rural charm and she noticed the old farm supply business had a quite a lot of properties for sale. She was soon at Maeve's house – a typical coastal weatherboard home which hadn't changed since Jill had last visited. She knocked on Maeve's front door, oddly a bright red door. Strange, she thought, she didn't remember Maeve having a red door.

"Why Jill, hello there," her sister said, giving her a warm hug. She wore brown linen pants, and a white shirt, with comfortable flats. Jill was surprised. She had remembered Maeve was one for sensible dressing which equated with light, shapeless dresses and homey pumps.

"Maeve, I'm fine. So good to see you again and thank you for having me…I really needed this holiday…"

Maeve put a gentle hand on her arm and guided her inside. There was an uncharacteristic gentleness in her face that was unfamiliar to Jill. The last time she'd seen Maeve was at Maeve's husband's funeral. She and Bill had travelled up together. Maeve had been in Western Australia visiting her daughter when Bill died and Jill had told her not to come all the way back to the funeral. It had been five years since Jill had seen her and the change was remarkable. She never remembered that Maeve was a free spirit, yet standing beside her sister now she had to admit she had softened. The doilies and the lace had gone, replaced by easy, comfortable furniture. In fact, as Jill looked around her, she saw a warm and inviting home and, as she looked at Maeve, she saw compassion and something else in her sister's face; she saw empathy.

"Sit down Jill and make yourself at home will you. I so rarely see you these days that it's wonderful to have you here, albeit under difficult circumstances," Maeve said.

Jill coughed, noticing that the stupid lump was beginning to build in her throat again. It was present most days now, a ball of unresolved grief that would dislodge at the most inappropriate times. It was at those times that Jill could not control the crying anymore. The community health nurse who came to visit her to 'assess' if she needed home help had said this uncontrollable crying was normal for someone who had lost their life partner. Normal! She hardly knew anymore what was normal and what was not. "Thank you Maeve for your hospitality…and your understanding as well. It has not been…easy of late."

"No problems whatsoever Jill. I'll make us a nice cup of something. Won't be a tick."

While she and her sister weren't close, they had never really fought, only discovered they weren't alike, but as Jill sat in her sister's comfortable, breezy lounge room, she had to admit that perhaps Maeve had undergone some radical experience that had left her changed. She looked at her in the kitchen; making dandelion coffee, and noticed the upended herbs she had hanging from her ceiling. "Maeve?" Jill said.

Her sister turned from the kitchen bench. She looked like she was chopping up fresh fruit. "Yes Jill."

"You're different to when you were married." And then correcting herself. "From when you were widowed."

Maeve turned around and it was then Jill noticed the

thing that was different about Maeve was her confidence. She was still the same person underneath but something had given way within her to reveal an assuredness Jill only vaguely remembered from childhood. She stopped cutting the fruit which she was piling into two bowls.

"Different? I suppose so Jill." She carried the coffee and fruit and placed them in front of Jill. "Help yourself dear. You must be feeling like you need some fresh food after the pies and sausage rolls of the train cafeteria. Go on tuck in."

Jill picked up a slice of watermelon and sipped at her coffee. She had to admit Maeve was right; she felt the need to eat healthily but she wasn't going to let Maeve off so easily. "Now don't go changing the subject Maeve. We should be able to speak frankly with each other. You *are* different. What's changed in you?"

Maeve sat back and crossed her legs, running her hand through her short grey curls which were usually styled at the hairdresser, though now they looked uncombed and a little wild.

"My hair. That's what's changed," she said. "Stopped going to the hairdressers after Rob died. Just didn't see the point."

"Umm," Jill said, letting the silence linger between them.

"And I can hear your thoughts whirring inside your head sister. You're wondering why I look and sound different."

Jill nodded. "Yes…I have to admit to that. Tell me Maeve, what happened to you."

Maeve's voice was full of compassion. "It's simple Jill. After Rob died I was forced to change because I became conscious of my own mortality. I could no longer afford to sit in my armchair with a cup of tea in front of me, staring into space and waiting for my turn to come. I wanted to get as much living as I could do in the time I had left."

She sat back in her chair a little shocked by the truth of Maeve's words. "I'm sorry. I wasn't around for you Maeve. I could have helped."

Her sister shook her head and placed a soft hand on hers. "Don't beat yourself up kiddo. I was always the oldest one, perhaps blazing the trail for you to follow."

"What do you mean Maeve? I'm ok. I don't need any radical changes."

"Don't you?" Maeve said. "You haven't come to see me in five years. You never travelled alone when Bill was alive, yet here you are – one long train trip and a bumpy bus ride later...What has happened to make you come here?"

Jill got up to clear the cups and take the half eaten fruit away, but Maeve got up too. She wasn't going to give up on getting the truth out of her sister so easily either. "Leave them Jill. Why are you here?" she said, trying to push the point.

She put the dishes in the sink and the two of them stood staring out to the huge backyard that led onto the rainforest. The golf ball lump hid in Jill's throat again waiting to be discovered. "Umm...I wanted to see you, yes. But I also needed time to think Maeve." She swallowed hard. "Umm...they want me to go into the retirement home...Golden Dreams Retirement Village...and I don't want to. I was hoping to find the strength here, away from them, to tell them I don't want that...don't need that...yet." Maeve put her arms around Jill's shoulders. "It's alright honey. You've come to the right place. We've got plenty of time and space here in this quiet corner of the world for you to think. You think all you need to, for as long as you need to, but Jill remember this...whatever you do, you must do on your own."

She looked at her sister then, puzzled by her words. "Alone. I must do this alone. What do you mean Maeve?"

"I can't help you find your feet Jill. As much as I would like to help, I can't. You must decide for yourself how you want to live. All your life you've waited for Bill to make your decisions, just as I waited for Rob. When he passed there was no-one to make them for me anymore and for a long time I just curled up in my bedroom and let the world pass me by. But as I learned to do things on my own and make my own decisions, I made a big discovery. Do you know what that was?"

Jill shook her head slightly. "I've no idea Maeve…"

"I discovered that I actually liked myself, and my life, and my freedom. Being widowed was not the end of the world for me. I discovered that I had to get busy living because I wasn't ready to die yet."

She began washing the cups out of habit. She liked a clean sink at all times of the day.

"Leave those Jill. I'll do them after tea," her sister said.

But she was impatient for the conversation to end. She didn't understand her sister; making decisions with Bill was a joy to her. She didn't need to 'find' herself…who she was without Bill? She only needed to regain her independence after Bill's passing because her children didn't trust her to be on her own, and she felt powerless to fight them.

She could hear the sounds of the rainforest and feel the warmth of the sun through the kitchen window. "It's ok Maeve. I'll do them. I like a clean sink."

4 A REVELATION

"Come on Jill. Are you ready yet?" Maeve had organised a car trip for the day to the nearby national park. She prayed there would be no walking. Maeve was a lot more fit than Jill, particularly with her hip problem; but she didn't protest when her sister suggested the trip. "Sure. That'd be nice. I love the rainforest." And she did. As they drove in Maeve's small All Wheel Drive, down back roads and through tree lined lanes, surrounded by green hills and patches of rainforest, she had to admit the trip was a good idea.

She had wound her window down so the soft morning sun could touch her bare arm. She had dressed simply that morning in a T-shirt and cotton pants. The loafers she never wore at home suited her laidback coastal fashion, and she felt comfortable and...free. Maeve had put on a sun dress, sandals and a straw hat. Jill marvelled at how far Maeve had come in the past few years. She no longer carried the weight of other people's expectations. She was her own woman.

The drive was refreshing and relaxing after the silence that had shrouded her home when Bill passed. Every room echoed with his memory and the fine dust that had begun to gather on her window sills gave the home a desolate feel. Here on the north coast with her sister, she felt herself begin to thaw.

"Maeve?"

"Yes?" Her sister replied, their comfortable communication of childhood beginning to return.

"Tell me about what it was like for you after Rob passed. How long did it take you to get on your feet?"

Maeve shifted into top gear. They had come to a relatively straight part of the road. Wild daisies grew on the roadside and the blue sky was dotted with faint white clouds. The colours of the landscape were vivid like a painting. "Umm, it's still not easy to go back there Jill, to those memories. It was a terrible time for me but I guess you understand that. Don't you?"

She nodded wordlessly.

"My Rob died suddenly, as you know. No time to prepare. One day we were eating tea together, the next I was staring at a vacant chair where he would have been sitting. I thought it was some sort of joke, that someone would come through the door and tell me Rob was down at the local pub and staying for one more beer. But no one came through the door, and the next night and the next, his chair was still vacant. I gave up eating at the table then. What was the point?"

"Yes. I've done that too," Jill said.

They were coming to the entrance of the national park.

"I think you're going to enjoy this Jill. Picked the spot specially for you, given I know you like the outdoors – and best of all it's a short walk to somewhere beautiful," Maeve said.

The car came to a halt and it was a short stroll, as promised, to the nearby waterfall. Jill could just glimpse it. Getting her walking stick out of the car, she waited for Maeve.

"I love it Maeve. Beautiful," she said.

Maeve joined her carrying the picnic basket, a rug and fold up chair for Jill. "Here you poor old thing, carry the rug," she said, merriment in her eyes. Jill felt good today with her sister, and soaking in the calm permanence of the old landscape. "Oh, and I love your stick Jill. It's actually a proper stick for walking, not a manufactured old person's cane."

"I know. I saw it in a rather bohemian little store in a nearby tourist town at home and thought if that's a walking stick then I have to have it."

They began to walk toward the falls. "Tell me Jill have you thought about the future, really? I know Jeff is pressuring you to go into the retirement village, but what about you. Have you given where you're going to live some serious thought?"

Jill took a deep breath of fresh air and was momentarily lost in her surroundings. "Yes. Well, no. Not really," she said, looking expectantly at Maeve hoping her older sister might have some answers.

"Don't look at me Jill for advice; I'm not you. I just know that I didn't want to move out of my marital home. Too many memories to be lost that way. Will you stay where you are?"

Jill shook her head. "I can't Maeve. I'm not like you. Every room I go into I expect to see Bill there. When it all boils down to it, our home was a home because he was there. I just feel...strongly...that there's something else for me, but I don't know what. Trouble is, that my children are worried enough to think they've got the right to pressure me into doing something I don't want to do. Old age Maeve; it's no picnic."

Maeve threw back her head and laughed like a teenager. That was one thing that hadn't changed about her sister and that was her ability to laugh loudly, and often. Jill smiled at her, understanding for the first time that perhaps she had sold Maeve short for years, and that she had missed out on so much from her sister, simply because it had been decreed at an early age they didn't get along. She understood now that she had competed with her sister for as long as she could remember and one of the reasons for it was Maeve's ability to find the right way to go about things...before Jill did.

They came to the waterfall, a cascading, bubbling pool that fed the nearby creek which wound its way through the rainforest. A grassy patch near the pool was an invitation to spread the picnic rug.

Maeve pulled out a Tupperware container full of cheese cubes and cabanossi. In her other hand was a container full of assorted savoury biscuits.

"Deeevine," Jill said, reaching in and gathering some cheese and meat, and a biscuit in the other hand. "Real, Aussie canapés."

"But that's not the lot," her sister said, "I have wine. Riesling of course. Just the one you like."

She poured Jill a generous plastic tumbler and a little less for herself, given she was driving.

"Ah, the memories of times past," Maeve said. "And I've done some living too Jill. Some of it you know, and some you don't."

She glanced at her sister wondering what prompted her comment. "What do you mean Maeve? I know all there is to know about you. We have no secrets."

Maeve leant back, staring past Jill to the waterfall. "I don't suppose I should be telling you this now Jill, but somehow I feel it's important to tell you. If there is one thing that comes with age it's knowing the right time for things…mainly because you know you haven't much time left."

"Go on," Jill said, wondering what on earth Maeve had kept hidden from her.

"…I'm sorry Jill we haven't been all that close over the years. You were hundreds of miles away. Our lives just went in different directions and you and Bill were so busy building your business…and your place in country society. On the other hand, I was busy finding my son…"

Jill began to interrupt but Maeve put her hand up to silence her. "Let me finish Jill. You didn't know did you? I gave up a child for adoption in my teens. Oh, don't worry you weren't the only one. Mum and dad made sure no-one knew. Not my family, the townsfolk, no-one. And I buried it deep too Jill, so deep I almost forgot my son, but never quite. The guilt of giving him up never left me. You wondered why I kept my distance all these years; it was because I could never forgive myself, because I had built up such a wall against the truth, that it was easier to stay away from people who knew my past."

Maeve sat in silence, never taking her eyes off the water as it flowed into the creek and began its journey to nourish the ground over which it ran. Jill didn't want to break that silence. She had always known there was something missing with her sister but she could never account for it. A vague knowing that her standoffish attitude was borne from a deep emotion and the wall she had built around it to keep people out.

And so they sat for the quietest of minutes with nothing but the call of the rainforest's birds and the bubbling sound of water to break their thoughts. Maeve turned to her sister with a look of gratitude which said: 'thank you for not judging me'.

"It was only when I knew my life was drawing to a close and I didn't want to take my secret to my grave that I went looking, Jill. Can you believe I waited all that time to find my son?"

Still Jill didn't speak but instead wordlessly encouraged her sister to say what needed to be said.

"So I found him, a middle aged man living on his own in a flat, on a pension. His life hadn't been blessed; he was not placed into a good home. While Rob and I were having children of our own and sacrificing to give them the best possible start in life, caring for them and making sure they were shielded from the harshness of life, my son had no-one. His parents were no good. He spent his life feeling something was missing but he never knew what. I wonder Jill what it's like to know deep down that there is a big, giant piece of the puzzle missing, and have no way to solve that puzzle. You must feel like life is having a huge laugh at your expense. Anyway, he turned to drugs and alcohol. When I found him he was dying of lung cancer. That's the thing, isn't it? When a person can't solve the riddles of life they just block them out. When the pain is buried so deep and enough silent tears have been cried, they give up…"

Jill placed her hand over her sister's to offer as much comfort as she could though she knew it was pointless. The guilt and pain of losing her son would never ease, never fade. It was a gaping wound that could not heal. "I'm so sorry Maeve. No-one deserved this. Not you as the young teenager forced to abandon your child, nor the son you never knew who couldn't rise above the unknowable pain he carried of not belonging."

Maeve dabbed at her eyes where the tears had gathered and were beginning to spill over, down her cheeks. "I don't suppose so Jill…but there's a reason why I told you this story now. My son is gone, passed last year, and I was at his side. I've made peace with my past and its legacy and, in the end; I made peace with my son. I found in that journey a way to let go of the past and that's what you must do. My story is my gift to you little sister. It's my way of saying that it's possible to face the pain of love and loss and go on."

It was Jill's turn to wipe away the tears. She didn't know if she was crying them for her sister and the nephew she never knew, or whether it was for the pain of losing Bill. She only knew they were deep, cleansing tears and, for the first time since Bill's death, she felt some of the weight of her grief lift.

"And now," Maeve said, her voice rough with emotion. "We should have a good, long drink."

They clicked their plastic glasses, took decent swigs of

the Riesling, and began to eat the corned meat sandwiches
Maeve had prepared earlier that morning.

5 HORIZONS

Jill let Maeve sleep and closed the side door slowly so as not to disturb her. They were both tired from the picnic and a sleep-in was the medicine needed to restore scattered emotions, but something had been playing on her mind since they returned from their day trip to the waterfall. She couldn't put her finger on it but she knew she needed to get to the sea, to walk on its shore and feel the ocean breeze. She wanted to look out at the horizon and find the answers she needed. It was a short drive to the coast, so she left Maeve a note to let her know where she'd be. Reversing Maeve's car slowly out of the driveway, so as not to wake her sister, she set off. Life had not been predictable since Bill's passing Jill thought, as she reflected on the past few months. Her hip ached from the walk to the falls but she pushed through the pain. She wanted to see the ocean and that's what she would do.

She pointed the car in the direction of the coast and drove. The roads were busy with traffic going to and from work, and she slowed down. She had been a good driver in her day but age had blunted her nerve and the pace of the roadways was, at times, overwhelming. She settled on an acceptable speed and gripped the steering wheel less tightly. She may as well enjoy the drive in unfamiliar territory. That was the thing she'd noticed since Bill's passing: there were so many new things to get used to; things she hadn't done for years, like pay a bill – her husband had taken care of that, or register her car. Bill had done that too. She now had to talk to the council people about the rate increases on their investment houses in town, and greet the water and electricity metre readers when they came. Even taking the garbage out. He had done so much.

She had almost panicked when it came to renewing the registration on her car. She found out how to book the car in for its pink slip, to haggle with the insurance company, and to gather all those things together and wait in the long queues at the motor registry. She had given so much control of the day to day things to Bill that she had forgotten how to be responsible. But she was relearning. She had to. It was all part of proving to her family she could stand on her own two feet – that she didn't need Golden Dreams Retirement Village. One day she might, but not yet. "And for as long as I can, I'll stay out of places like that," she said aloud. Well maybe not to thin air, she thought. There was always the feeling that Bill was near to her. He was in the constant swarm of butterflies in her path, no matter where she walked, and the flock of birds that took flight at sunset and in that little bird's song.

She reached the concrete car park of the beach and stopped the car, noticing with relief the beach was relatively deserted. She kicked off her sandals. She would walk with bare feet and scrunch the sand between her toes. She left her walking stick in the car; if she headed for the shoreline, that part of the beach where the water hardened the sand, she would be alright and the walking would not cause her too much pain. Her hip was sensitive to uneven ground.

She made her way, slowly, to the shoreline and glanced up and down the long beach. She took her hair out of its bun and let it fly loose. She had always loved the feel of long hair, no matter what her age. The ocean breeze blew at the thin cotton of her skirt and she held it down with her hands. The last thing anybody needed was to see her legs, she thought with a smile. The sea was a little rough and the swirling currents reminded her of her life over the past few months. So much had changed; so much was in flux; so much needed resolving.

She walked round the curved shoreline until the far off inlet became a small lake. She stopped at its shore noticing several fishermen had thrown in their lines and were waiting for a catch.

"Beautiful day today, isn't it?" and older gentleman called.

She nodded and waved, hoping this would do without the need to talk further, but the fisherman was not going to give up that easily.

"You're not from around here are you?" he said. There was nothing for her to do but walk up to him and answer his question. She was slightly annoyed at his presence. She had wanted to be alone with her thoughts, not interrupted by a stranger's polite prattle.

"No," she said, "just enjoying a walk by the sea. Caught anything yet?"

He laughed, as if the joke was on her. "No, 'fraid not. I never do."

She was puzzled, and couldn't resist the ambiguity of his reply. "Well then, why do you waste your time fishing here if you don't catch anything? That doesn't make any sense."

He pulled at his line, as if testing to see if there was a bite. "It's not the catching I like; it's the anticipation of the catch I might get. Understand?"

"Not really," she said, truthfully. She took a second glance at the man. He seemed about her age, short and wiry and unlike Bill who was tall and commanding. She wondered why he was so intent to engage her in conversation, and went to leave.

"Look I don't know your name, but it's not every day a woman your age comes walking along the beach alone with a look that says she's lost as all hell."

Her eyes widened with the shock of his directness. "I

beg your pardon?"

"You heard," he said stubbornly, as though politeness was a vague notion he never entertained.

Her temper flared. She might be alone but she didn't have to take rudeness from a stranger. And how did he know she was alone anyway? "What makes you think I'm alone? My family, my husband could be just over that sand dune."

He looked in the direction of the nearby beach, and shook his head. "I don't think so. You have a look, like me."

"And what's that look?"

"Well, you look like you're missing something...or someone."

She relaxed then. Somehow, this strange fisherman had picked up her aloneness and, perhaps, her confusion. She gave him her full attention.

"You're right. I lost my husband a few months back. And you?"

"...My wife, about a year ago. I would say I'm less alone than you're feeling at the moment. But the sea's a good tonic. It's so big and we're so small. It seems to take our troubles into its depths and kind of, hide them, for a while at least. That's why I come here and don't care if I catch anything. It's enough to just be here."

Jill moved towards the man. "I'm Jill Bridges. Nice to meet you. I'm sorry if I was a bit standoffish before..."

He extended his hand to her. "James E Howard. The E stands for Eric by the way. I live just up there." He pointed to a wooden cabin that hugged the rugged rocks above the beach. "Got a view all the way to the horizon."

"Umm...sounds lovely," she said, shaking his hand. "I don't live here. I come from a little town south east of Sydney. About four hour's drive from the city. I'm here visiting my sister in Wauchope."

He shifted his weight onto his other foot and she

thought she saw a flicker of pain cross his face. "Do you want to sit down," she said, pointing to the grassy knoll at the end of the sand dune.

"That'd be fine with me…Jill. Had my hip replaced six months ago and I'm still getting used to the new one. I'm not as young as I used to be," he said, with just a hint of a twinkle in his eyes.

She laughed. "I'll second that one James E Howard." Jill felt uncommonly at ease with her newly acquired acquaintance now, so she encouraged the conversation flow. She didn't know why but it felt good to be yarning to someone who didn't know her, nor her past, or Bill.

They sat down - well more leaned against the knoll - both gazing toward the horizon. "I love the ocean," she said, breaking the silence. "It calms my thoughts…I don't think about the future, just the moment and that beautiful horizon."

"I'm an ocean man myself. Love it. Used to live in the big cities…you know, had my own business but when it came to retirement, I just wanted out. Spot of fishing and the sea; that's all I wanted…after I lost my wife."

She leant in closer. "I'm so sorry James E. I know what that's like. It's been hard losing Bill after 40 years."

He placed a gnarled brown hand on hers. She wasn't offended by it. It seemed the most natural thing for him to do. "I'm sorry too…How long are you staying with your sister?"

He withdrew his hand and she folded her arms, leaning back again so her back was against the grass mound. "I'm here for another three weeks. Wanted to make it a decent stay, so I can have a good look round. I'm half considering buying a small property here."

"It's a pretty place for sure. I've never been happier, really. What about your family?"

She laughed. "Best not mention that one James E. They're trying to get me to go into a retirement home. I'm

MARYANN WESTON

not ready for that yet. Not for a long time."

"Yeah, I'll go down fighting on that one too. Look, I don't mean to be too forward but would you like to have a bite to eat with me tonight?"

She went to stand up. The conversation had taken an alarming turn in a direction she didn't want to go in. It wasn't right. "Ah...no, I mean...I don't mean to be rude...but I'm staying with my sister as I said. Wouldn't want to leave her alone."

She noticed he had green eyes which crinkled round the corners with a secret amusement only he seemed to know. "Now don't go getting upset Jill. It's only dinner I asked you to, not to share my cabin."

She blushed bright red, something she hadn't done since teenage years.

"Anyhow, why don't you bring this sister of yours? There's a nice place on the corner of the main street. No surprises that it serves the freshest seafood in town given it's also right on the beach. What do you say Jill? Can I tempt you?"

She smiled to ease the tension that was beginning to form in her jaw. "Tempt me? Well I must say James E Howard that I've enjoyed our little chat. Enjoyed it so much that it took my mind off my worries. I think it would be safe to say yes, and I'll bring my sister Maeve Woods. She's a lovely lady. You might know her?"

He shook his head. "No, but it doesn't matter. I hardly know you either and yet here we are taking things one step further than a brief catch up on the beach."

The tension returned. He was making her feel decidedly uncomfortable.

"You mean taking our acquaintance one step further...in any case it would be nice for Maeve and I to get out. 7pm tonight?"

He smiled, much like he might have if he'd caught a fish she thought. "Yep. Dories is the name of the restaurant.

Your sister will know it. Now can I walk you back to your car?"

"That would be nice James E," she said, helping gather his fishing tackle. "We can walk on the shoreline."

He nodded. "Only way to do it."

And they both walked down towards the sea, she with a slight limp due to her right hip, and he with a similar gait because of his left hip.

6 DINNER WITH JAMES E

Her sister Maeve was not easily surprised but Jill succeeded when she arrived home that afternoon, to tell her that they were both dining with James E Howard that night. "What on earth...where did you meet this man?"

So Jill explained the chance meeting and the dinner invitation. "I still don't know why I accepted. It's so uncharacteristic of me. I just don't do these things but he was a nice man. We had a lot in common and I thought about how long it had been since I'd made a new friend. You know Maeve, once you hit 50 the world contracts. Horizons don't expand anymore and the new people and influences start to fade. The meeting was so unexpected, and he was so insistent...I don't know. Maybe we'll enjoy a night out?" she offered.

"Well I have to say his choice of restaurant is good. We'll certainly enjoy our meal, if nothing else."

And so they had busied themselves getting ready for most of the afternoon. Maeve had chosen drill pants and a soft white over shirt. Jill had opted for a flowing caftan outfit, notable for the bright swirl of colours and shapes. They both felt quite proud they had reflected the laid back, coastal atmosphere in their dress that night. It had been years since they had gone out together, and they giggled like teenagers when they entered the restaurant.

Jill pointed James E Howard out. He too dressed in blues and whites, like an upmarket sailboat captain. He was right when he said he loved the sea.

"James, this is my sister Maeve. She's really your neighbour. Wauchope is definitely local."

He was warm and welcoming and Jill decided on the spot she hadn't made a mistake in accepting the invitation after all. They ordered oysters to start, followed by mud crabs and the catch of the day.

"Dessert ladies?"

They both declined. Far too much rich food had dented their appetite.

The conversation over coffee flowed. It was like the three had known each other for years.

"So tell me James, what did you do when you lived in the city?" Maeve asked.

He sat back, relaxed and sipping a black coffee and a small port. "I was in real estate actually Maeve. Always had a good eye for a bargain and I was just one of those people that can pick the right time and the right place. Started off with a small real estate business in Hurstville but when the south coast started to take off, I opened offices all the way down to Wollongong. I made a lot of money but I also made a lot of enemies too. It's not a world I would like to go back to; in fact I'm very happy with my log cabin overlooking the beach."

Maeve was sympathetic. "Yes, Rob and I worked hard all our lives in our own business and made some money but you can never get the hours back that you should have spent at home with your families can you?"

Jill nodded. "Yes, we used to get the babysitters in for the kids after five o'clock because we were still working at the business. All the growing up we missed that is gone in the blink of an eye."

James E Howard lent back in the chair. "So ladies, are we agreed?"

They both looked at him and Maeve asked: "About what?"

He took a slow sip of his coffee before answering. "That life's too short to waste. That we're here for a short time and the older we get, the more we realise we can't waste our time, not for a second. Port ladies?"

They both nodded, with a smile.

With dinner finished, James E invited them both to the beach the next day for fishing...well to learn how to fish. It's not something Jill had ever tried and it had been years since Maeve had fished with Rob.

Surprising herself, Jill accepted while Maeve held back. "Oh I don't know James E. I'm not one for the beach really. That's why I live on the hinterland."

It took both Jill and James E ganging up on her like school kids in a playground to eventually get her to cave in under pressure. On the drive home Maeve was thoughtful. "What's going on little sister?"

Jill stared out the window at the fading light. The landscape was unfamiliar to her, so unlike the rural countryside of her home, but it did not feel alien. She was surprised by that; she could come to another part of the country, alone and without Bill, and feel strangely at home. "I don't know Maeve. I met a nice man on the beach today, around my age and he invited us to dinner. It's no more than that but I did enjoy the evening out. It's been so...empty, lonely...since Bill passed. And I'm conscious now, more than ever, that my time here on this earth is finite. I'm not sure I want to go back to my old life. More and more it's feeling like I need to close that book, start afresh..."

"Move? Are you seriously considering moving away from the home you've been in for 40 years? Do you know what that will involve?"

"Well, hopefully, better times than I've had since Bill passed. Look Maeve, my son and daughter have their own lives. Aside from Sara Jane, young people aren't much interested in being around an 'old person'. And anyway, it seems everyone wants me in a retirement home. I'm not going there Maeve. I'm not. Into a one bedroom flat to watch television all day, or see my housemates die one by one, knowing my turn is soon. There's got to be more to living than that?"

She felt Maeve's silent support in the growing darkness. "I know dear. I know. It's only that I've been so dominating that my family haven't suggested the same for me...but there will come a time when it will be me farewelling old friends and wondering when it's my turn. You know I used to visit an old friend in one of the local retirement home's here. In his day, he was a fine actor and started the drama theatre here. Oh many plays were produced to entertain the people of Wauchope. And many a young kid got a good start in theatre because of him. That theatre went for 60 years but after his wife passed he eventually had to move out of his home. It was only the theatre community that used to visit him in the early days but even they dropped off. But, you know, every time I went to see him I would get halfway down the hallway and I would hear this tap, tap. It was my friend typing on his old typewriter still writing plays until the end, and I was the only visitor. That tap tap was the only thing that filled his days. Sad isn't it?"

"I never want that to happen to me," she said, staring at the blackness outside the car. She shivered. She felt like she had the weight of the world on her shoulders. In any case, for a few short weeks she could make new friends, and get to know this new country which was drawing her into its green valleys and blue seas.

7 FISHING

They did go fishing the next day, and the day after that. In fact Maeve began to get quite good at it, while Jill sat under the umbrella on her deck chair reading her murder mystery. James E Howard was thrilled to have two students in his company because he could talk fishing for hours on end quite legitimately, given he was instructing them. The sun drenched days melded into one long holiday and Jill began to forget her grief, if only for an hour or two before she remembered.

One sunny day, shortly before she was due to board the south bound train home, James E asked her what she planned to do. They were standing at the sea shore, fishing lines caste into the blue green waters, with nothing to do but contemplate the horizon and wait for the fish to bite.

"I don't know James E. I love my family and I don't want to be away from them but I know my life can't continue the way it's been since Bill passed. There are alternatives but none I really like...completely."

"What about moving here? I know the real estate. There's another cabin up the road from me going cheap. If you make an offer on it within the next few weeks, there's a good chance you'll get it. I'm not trying to influence you...but give it some thought will you? You look a whole lot happier today than you did when I first met you."

She was grateful for his support but her mind was awash with indecision. "Not now James E. I have some thinking to do."

He turned to her, his face serious with the things he

wanted to say but could not.

"Look Jill, I have no right to be so frank with you. We've only known each other a few weeks but it's been long enough to know that your future doesn't include a retirement home just yet; it lies in living, really living. In waking up and being wild if you want to, in seeing the mischief in life and in grabbing this…" He waved his hand across the ocean and the shore, "with both hands and holding it while you can. Whatever you do, whatever you decide, don't give up on living Jill because life, all life, is precious and meant to be lived. We don't know how much time any of us have left but we do know we have this moment, and that's worth a lifetime of lost moments."

She nodded, the familiar lump was forming in her throat but she swallowed hard. She liked James E and she acknowledged the wisdom of his words.

"I will go back home the day after next James E and I will talk with my family. I don't know what I should do. I only hope that the answer will come to me, like a bottle washed up from the blue sea. And when it does, I'll know. I'll know what I should do."

He didn't speak, instead turning his concentration to his fishing and the waiting.

Jill said her goodbyes to Maeve and was sad to leave the sister she had only just gotten to know…and like. She promised to come back soon; and she resolved to try and move on from her grief. Jeff was at the station to pick her up. They drove home in relative silence after the perfunctory hellos. Since their conversation about Golden Dreams Retirement Village a wall had been built between them. She was on one side, shocked her son could suggest such a fate for her and had so little understanding of the person she was…still was. He was on the other side only wanting what was best for his mum; that she be safe and secure, and well cared for. He couldn't do that for her in his home. His wife Narelle worked and the children were so young. The retirement village was the best option and Jill knew he was wishing her stubborn resistance would just disappear.

She didn't invite him in for coffee, saying she was tired. "Let's talk in the morning dear."

He nodded and kissed her softly on the cheek. No matter what had come between them, he loved her dearly and was worried about her. "I love you mum. You know that?"

She kissed her son back. "It's alright darling. Come over for breakfast before you go to work. I'll make your special omelette." That was enough to make him smile.

"Absolutely mum. I'm there. See you then."

She watched the red tail lights disappear into the darkness that shrouded the street. She was tired as she walked up her front path and her hip was playing up in the cooler climate. She thought she heard the little bird sing its song and wondered who it had sung to in her absence. The empty house loomed and she knew would go straight to her bedroom and shut the door against the loneliness that surrounded her.

Jill slept fitfully that night, with the ghosts of yesterday visiting. In her dreams she was a young girl again walking beside Bill in the town's streets, and then she saw herself by his graveside. She was glad when the sun's rays broke through the dark to start the day. Then she remembered Jeff would be coming soon for breakfast before work.

She got up, dressed quickly and went to the kitchen, opening the backdoor to let the freshness of the morning in. She put the kettle on and whisked the eggs for Jeff's favourite, omelette with fresh tomato on the side. She turned to the small kitchen table where Bill usually sat and set a place for his son. Everywhere she looked the memories of her old life crowded in. She sighed and called for the little bird to sing his song. It was a reminder of the simple joy in life that could strike at the heart of life's complexity.

Her life needed to be lived like that, she thought. Simply and for each moment, not in the past and God knows not in the future but, day by day, and with a will to get the most out of the time she had left.

On her last day in Wauchope she had walked down to the local real estate agent on a whim, and not really knowing why. There she had seen the cabin James E had talked about. It had three bedrooms and was considerably smaller than her home, but that smallness was attractive to her. She had no wish to rattle around in a big house by herself any more. Once it had been a home with Bill and where they'd raised their children. But their children had grown up and made lives of their own. Realistically, she knew her place in their lives was limited. She would be invited for Sunday lunches, picked up from Golden Dreams and then taken back in the afternoon. They would drop by once during the week, perhaps midweek, and have a cup of tea with her. She would have biscuits for the children and treats for them so they would remember their visit and look forward to the next ones.

They would chat with the nursing staff and ask them how she was doing, and they would tell her family when she didn't take her pills, or had trouble with her bowels or, worse, when the forgetfulness had become dementia.

Jill saw the lonely years stretching out before her. Grey, lifeless years, with no real joy or self-affirmation. The kettle was whistling on the stove so she pulled it off and poured the hot water into the coffee machine Bill had given her the Christmas before last. She poured the eggs into the pan and ran a fork through them. She lifted two plates out of the cupboard and cut up the tomatoes. The hot toast popped and she put it on the plate, spreading the butter over it until it melted into the warm brown-ness.

The real estate agent had taken her on an inspection of

the cabin. She had loved the house from the moment she stepped into it. It was a wooden framed home, with a deck out the back that overlooked the ocean. The front room with its large timber framed cedar windows also caught an ocean breeze, as did the whole of the house. A small, but bright kitchen was decorated in yellow. The ocean breeze blew through the entire house. She stood and looked out to sea. Here, she knew she would find peace and independence. She had travelled back to Wauchope that evening not mentioning her trip to Maeve. Not that she wanted to keep secrets but she needed time to think...weigh the consequences and make decisions.

There was a knock at the backdoor. She looked up from her thoughts and waved to her son.

"Jeff, come in darling." She stood on her tip toes to kiss his cheek. She remembered the time when she had to stoop to kiss the top of his head.

"Hello mum. It's so good to have you back. I've missed you."

She spooned the eggs over the toast and laid out the plates on the table. "Come on, food's getting cold."

She poured her son a coffee. "How's the business going? And Narelle, the new baby and Sara Jane?"

"Good mum...good," he said between mouthfuls. "They're all missing you, you know...especially Sara Jane."

"Yes I missed them too. I'll drive out later this afternoon to say hello. Aunty Maeve sends her love."

He looked up from his food. "God it's been years since we've seen her. I'm really glad you went to visit her...reconnect with her. Hope she can come down and see us sometime."

Jill sat down with her son and began to eat her eggs but she didn't have much of an appetite.

"Oh mum, I meant to tell you that I've arranged for us to go out and look at Golden Dreams. I've put your name down on the waiting list. Hope that's ok? This house…it's just too big for you, and I worry…"

She put her fork down. "Jeff there's something I've been meaning to talk to you about."

He looked up from his breakfast. "This sounds serious mum…what's up?"

"No, it's not serious Jeff but it's important…The visit to Golden Dreams. It's not going to happen son. I'm not moving into a retirement home…well at least not yet."

"Mum you can't stay here. You and I both know this place is way too big for you. With your hip, being on your own…I don't want anything to happen to you…"

"More coffee?" she suggested, interrupting him mid sentence. He nodded, waiting for her to sit down again.

She topped up their coffee cups, pausing at the kitchen window. Outside the jasmine she planted with Bill was giving off its perfume. She would miss that, and her family.

"Darling…while I was away I had a lot of time to think. You're absolutely right. This house is too big for me, and it was our house – Dad and me – and I've just got no desire to stay here and live amongst memories. I rattle about here using only the bedroom and bathroom, the kitchen and my old easy chair over there. The rest of the time, I live with the ghosts of times past. It's no way to live Jeff…"

"Which is why I want you to go to Golden Dreams. God mum, you'll be around other people, have your own flat, and be close to care…"

"And sickness, and dementia, and people who have nowhere else to go. Let's face it Jeff, no-one is clamouring to go into an old people's home. You must know that."

He shook his head. "I don't understand you mum. You could come to me and Elle if you want. We could take it turnabout. Is that what you want?"

Jill shook her head, knowing that living with her children would not be good for her, or them. She never wanted to be a burden on anyone. She was far too proud for that.

"No son. I'm not coming to live with you or Elle. Not now, not ever."

"But where mum?"

"I've been thinking about moving up with Maeve. Not in with her, but near her. She's my sister and I haven't spent nearly enough time with her over the past 30 years. I've been too busy with you children. And I've loved doing that Jeff, really I have. I wouldn't take that time back for the world but you and Elle have your own lives now. Your own families, careers, and I…well now your dad has gone, I don't have anyone who needs me anymore."

He pushed his chair back and leant forward. She could see the faintest trace of frustration in his face, as though he was talking to a child who knew no better than to argue with an adult.

"That's just not true mum. I need you. Elle needs you. We all need you."

"I know darling. Don't get mad with me. Just try if you can to put yourself in my shoes. Now listen to me, really listen. Just imagine you are old and Narelle has passed. You've lost everything, your business, the love of your life, your health…You wake up every morning with pain and you rely on Sara Jane's visits to put the light in your life. You've lost the thing that you hold most dear, your independence. And your daughter is worried about you. She's talking about a retirement village. You don't want to go…not yet…while you still have your health and a sane mind. You know the time you have left on this earth is short, and you want to do some living, enjoy the precious years you have left. What do you do Jeff?"

He lowered his head. "Don't put it like that mum. No-one's trying to take your independence from you."

"I know. But the time has come for decisions Jeff, and I've found a little house up on the coast, near Maeve. I want to move there. In fact, I've put an offer in on the house...Now don't look hurt Jeff. You and the family can come up and have holidays by the sea...anytime...as often as you like. And I promise...I will spend no less than two months each year visiting you here. One month with you and one month with Elle. Mid-year and Christmas, and in January you come to me, and any time in between."

"I don't know mum. I can't stop you." He looked deep into her eyes, then away again, as if trying to understand why she was telling him she was going. The morning sun on the back veranda drew his attention and he sat for a moment in thought. She didn't interrupt him, knowing he was considering her words.

"Son?"

He turned to her and she saw his eyes were wet with tears. "Mum...don't go."

8 LIFE, LOVE AND LESSONS

The sea sparkled with the sun's rays coming off the swell of the blue-green waves. White tips broke the pattern as the ocean rose to meet the shore, giving way and breaking, to the delight of the children playing in its shallows.

Squeals of excitement rose above the boom of the waves and as Jill looked out from her deck chair, she marvelled at the sight of her grandchildren experiencing the simple joy the beach so generously offered. Sitting beside her were Elle and James E, and they were expecting Maeve for dinner that night. On the beach Jeff and Narelle chased their children endlessly around the shoreline.

"So mum, its paradise here," Elle said, sipping her cocktail. "And I must say Mr Howard, these cocktails are great."

James E grinned, pleased to be able to do something for Jill's family that made it easier for them to accept him. She had been seeing him for almost a year now. At first it started as a friendship but lately...well there was something more. She was resisting this, though, thinking that people of her age just didn't find love twice in their lives, and especially in their twilight years.

"I might go up and put on the barbecue Jill. What do you reckon?"

She nodded, smiling, glad he was here with her family.

"That would be wonderful. Thank you James E."

Elle waited until he was out of earshot. "Tell me mum, why do you call him James E and not James? Seems funny;

sounds a bit funny…"

She smiled. "Now Elle don't go getting conservative on me because I know you're not. I call him that because it's so different from your dad's name. You know no-one will ever replace your dad."

She nodded and reached for her mother's hand. They had become closer since Jill had moved to the coast. She wasn't sure why. Whether it was because they saw less of each other, or because Jill had stepped out into her own identity. She was no longer Bill Bridges' wife, or Jeff and Elle's mother, instead she was a woman like Elle, only at a different stage of her life.

"Do you think Jeff has gotten used to me being here Elle?" she said, raising the thing that had preoccupied her mind for the most of the year.

"I don't know mum. I really don't. He often says he thinks you should be back home but then I see him reading your letters and he's smiling. Sometimes he says to me, 'she's really happy isn't she?' And I tell him yes and that's the main thing. Honestly, I think he's happy if you're happy. He just misses you, that's all."

"I know dear. I know. But there're always the trade-offs in life aren't there? The trick is to find the solution that is best for everyone and causes the least amount of pain and suffering. There was always going to be that; whether it was for your children seeing the life leave my eyes in that home, or wondering after I'm gone if you'd done the right thing by putting me into the retirement home. The point is…well the point is that I am happy, and we are together today, here and now…and besides, it's Christmas tomorrow."

Elle squeezed her hand. "It's going to be alright with Jeff. Really it is mum. Don't worry about him."

Jill felt the water spray as her grandchildren chased each other nearby. She put her hands up. "Hey you two," but they were out of earshot running down to the water again, squealing as they chased each other. Narelle stayed at the shoreline to keep watch while Jeff took a break. He arrived at their little beach camp of deck chairs, umbrellas and towels panting from the effort of chasing his children.

"Not as young as I once was," he said. Jill handed him a towel. "No darling, none of us are."

He sat down beside her. "Enjoying yourself?" she asked.

"Yes mum, we're having a great time here with you." He looked across the beach and out to the horizon. "How could we not?"

"Oh, I just wondered. It's important to me that both you and Elle are right with me living here. And with James E being in my life."

Jeff shrugged, remaining silent but Elle was not going to let him off that easily.

"Come on younger brother," she said, giving him a shove so that he nearly fell sideways into the sand.

"Ok," he said, recovering his balance. "I'm fine with it."

She looked into his blue eyes; the same colour as his father's. "Really?"

"Yes really mum," he said, not turning away from his mother's question. She kept her directness up for just a moment before looking out to sea towards the horizon, satisfied finally with her son's answer.

Somewhere, far away from the coast, a little bird was heading north towards the warmer weather carrying his song for someone else. It would sing for them because it needed to, because they needed to know…that it did not have an answer to life's burdens; only a song for them in those wakeful hours before dawn and that song was about life.

ABOUT THE AUTHOR

Maryann Weston is a professional writer, training initially as a journalist and editor.

She has made it her mission to follow her dreams, including writing novels, and has combined her love of new challenges and new horizons with a vivid imagination and ability to tell a good story.

Maryann has a Bachelor of Communications (Journalism) and is also a qualified teacher and counsellor, with a Graduate Diploma in Education and a Diploma of Community Services.

She currently works as a journalist, editor and public relations professional and is a mum to three boys. She lives with her family in rural NSW, Australia.

Maryann also writes action/adventure books for teenagers including Shadowscape and Dawn of the Shadowcasters.

You can follow Maryann Weston on Twitter @MaryannWeston, on Facebook at Imagine If – Maryann Weston Books, follow her blog at www.extrasensitiveperson.wordpress.com or visit her website www.maryannwestonbooks.weebly.com

MARYANN WESTON

www.ingramcontent.com/pod-product-compliance
Lightning Source LLC
Chambersburg PA
CBHW070324130626
46556CB00007B/2719